HALLAM

A LUCAS HALLAM SHORT FICTION COLLECTION

L.J. WASHBURN

ROUGH
EDGES
PRESS

Hallam
Print Edition
© Copyright 2022 (As Revised) L.J. Washburn

Rough Edges Press
An Imprint of Wolfpack Publishing
5130 S. Fort Apache Rd. 215-380
Las Vegas, NV 89148

roughedgespress.com

Paperback ISBN 978-1-68549-055-3

HALLAM

HALLAM

This is the first appearance of Hallam, a cowboy who has outlived the days of the old west to become a gun-toting private eye and stuntman in the early days of motion pictures in California.

HALLAM WAITED BEHIND THE ROCKS, Colt Cavalry Model .45 gripped firmly in his big right hand. The riders would be here soon and he could go to work. For now, though, he waited. Seemed like that was all he did most of the time since he got into this crazy business.

The clatter of hooves came to his keen ears and he straightened, body taut now with expectation. He was a big man, tall and wide-shouldered, looking right at home in the buckskins and wide-brimmed hat. A full cartridge belt was fastened around his lean hips. Besides the holster for the .45, a sheathed Bowie knife was suspended from it.

The bone handle of the Colt felt good in his calloused palm, rekindled a lot of memories. If he let his mind drift, it seemed almost like he was back in the old days. The days when Lucas Hallam was a respected— and feared—name in Texas and New Mexico and Arizona...

"Get ready, Lucas. They're almost here. Steady now... Action!"

Vaguely, Hallam heard the director's commands and obeyed them like the professional he was. But as he swung around the rocks into the open, the rolling thunder of racing hoof beats filling his ears, he might have been home again.

"Hold it!" he roared, lining the Colt on the group of riders. There was no sound on this picture, of course, but the words came out anyway.

The riders pulled back on the reins and slowed their mounts to a stop. There were five of them, all wearing cowboy clothes and big hats. Bright bandannas were tied around the lower halves of their faces. The men were hard-eyed, glaring at the big man who faced them down without even a hint of fear in his manner.

From his post beside the camera, the director called, "Now. Jerry, go for your gun!"

One of the men on horseback, one who was dressed all in black, sent his hand streaking for the butt of the pistol holstered on his hip. To Hallam's eyes, the draw was pitifully slow, and he had to concentrate in order not to shoot too soon. He let the black-clad actor get his gun all the way out, waited until the muzzle was swinging into line with him.

Then Hallam squeezed the trigger of his own gun,

felt the familiar buck against the palm of his hand. Smoke blossomed from the barrel.

The gunman on the horse dropped his pistol and clutched his stomach. His face distorted in mock pain.

"Now ride!" the director shouted.

All of the men urged their horses forward, even the one who was supposed to be wounded. Hallam triggered off a couple of shots, then darted out of the way. The horses galloped past him. He fired after the fleeing men, but they didn't slow down until they were well out of camera range.

"Cut! That was great, fellas, just great!"

Hallam took a deep breath and slid the long-barreled Colt back in its holster. Playtime was over. With the rolling gait of a man who has spent a lot of his life on the back of a horse, he walked toward the long table where a couple of girls were handing mil lemonade to the actors. The California sun was hot this time of day, made a man thirsty.

Before he reached the table, though, the director hurried up to him and stopped him. "Great take, Lucas!" he said, he looked speculatively up at the foot-taller Hallam. "You've got star quality. Why do you want to keep on being an extra? You could be as big as Tom Mix if you wanted to. Why, you'd leave Gibson and McCoy and all the rest behind!"

Hallam shook his head. "I'm no actor, Bernie," he said simply. "Just a broke-down old cowboy."

"Yeah, sure. And I'm D.W. Griffith. Listen, Lucas—"

Hallam shook his head with a smile and turned away. The director had made this pitch to him before. Working as an extra got Hallam through the lean times when his agency wasn't attracting any clients, but being a movie star was the last thing he wanted.

Too much hoopla mixed up with that. Wouldn't sit well with a man like him.

There was another interruption before he made it to the lemonade. A long black car pulled up behind the trucks of the movie company. The driver got out, asked a question of a passing script girl. The girl pointed to Hallam.

Hallam saw the exchange and watched the man striding toward him. The newcomer was big, too, but he wore a pin-striped suit and a pulled-down Panama instead of cowboy clothes.

He stopped in front of Hallam, looked him up and down in disbelief, and said, "You're a private dick?"

"I'm Lucas Hallam, if that's who you're lookin' for." Hallam felt an instant dislike for this man, but he kept his voice flat and impassive.

The man jerked a thumb over his beefy shoulder. "Somebody wants to see you, Hallam."

"Question is, do I want to see this somebody?"

The man stiffened. He wasn't used to people asking questions. "You wanna see him if you know what's good for you, Tex," he snapped.

Hallam rubbed his jaw, squinted toward the long black car. He could see a figure sitting in the back seat. "Maybe your boss should do his own askin'," he said slowly.

"Why, you moth-eaten old bastard—" the man hissed. His hand shot out and clamped down on Hallam's shoulder. "You'll come when I tell you to come, you—"

Hallam hit him in the stomach with his left and jerked his shoulder loose. His right swept around as the man gasped and took a step backward. The blow cracked into his jaw and knocked him sprawling. With a growled curse, he reached under his coat and grabbed an automatic out of a shoulder rig.

Just as the gun came clear, the man froze, the point of Hallam's Bowie knife resting easily just under his chin. The blade barely pricked the skin, but it was enough to stop any threat the man wanted to make.

Hallam smiled down at him.

"This ain't a prop, son," Hallam said so softly the man could barely hear him. "You go to movin' too much, it'll slice your head right off. Now take that gun out real slow and put it on the ground."

A crowd was gathering around the two men, but nobody got too close as the man followed Hallam's orders. This wasn't playacting, and everybody knew it.

A voice cut through the tension. "Very impressive, Mr. Hallam. I'll thank you to let my man up now, though."

Hallam kept the knife where it was. He looked up to see who had spoken, saw a slim man of medium height wearing a lightweight white suit. Everything about him said money, from the carefully cut sandy hair to the Italian shoes on his feet.

Hallam straightened from his crouch and stepped back from the man he had knocked down. The knife went into its sheath. "Need to teach your people better manners, mister," Hallam rumbled.

"You're probably right, Mr. Hallam. I assume that you *are* Lucas Hallam?"

"That's right. Who're you?"

The man extended his hand. "Anthony Rose. I have a job for you, Mr. Hallam, and I'd like to discuss it with you."

Hallam's big hand briefly engulfed Rose's smaller one. "I'll talk to you. Won't say I'll take the job just yet, though."

"Fair enough," Rose replied. "Were you through for the day?"

Hallam looked at the director and got a quick, nervous nod. Bernie knew who Anthony Rose was, just as well as Hallam did.

"Seem to be."

"Good. I'll give you a ride back to town, then."

The big man in the pin-stripes had gotten up by now and was standing nearby, looking murderously at Hallam. He kept his mouth shut, though, and made no move to start more trouble.

"Let's go, Bert," Rose said to him, and the man hurried to the car to open the back door.

The car was big enough that even Hallam, with his long legs, was able to sit comfortably in the back seat next to Rose. The windows were down, and Hallam took off his hat and let the cool breeze ruffle his shaggy gray hair. It felt good after the heat and dust of location shooting.

Rose looked over at Hallam in his buckskins and said, "You don't look like any private detective I ever saw."

"Man's got to eat," Hallam said. "Movie work pays good."

"So do I. Do you know who I am, Mr. Hallam?"

"Course I do." Hallam paused. "You're one of the biggest crooks on the West Coast."

For a moment, Rose seemed on the verge of anger. In the front seat, the pin-striped Bert gaped in amazement that anybody would talk to his boss like that, especially some goofy old cowboy.

Then Rose chuckled and said, "Take us to the *Gilded Lily*, Bert. I'll do my talking there." He turned to his companion in the back seat. "I think you're just the man for this job, Hallam. We're going to get along fine."

"We'll see," Hallam said.

———

ROSE MADE small talk during the drive to Los Angeles and the ride in an expensive motor launch out beyond the limit, out to the *Gilded Lily*. Hallam had never been to the gambling ship, but he had heard stories about it. It was only one of Rose's enterprises; a fleet of smaller, quicker ships ran in tons of Mexican booze every year under Rose's direction. The *Gilded Lily* was his pride and joy, though, the place where he could play at being the little tin god he fancied himself.

Hallam had been told all that by friends on the LA force, but now he was seeing it firsthand. The sun was setting by the time they reached the ship, and it was already ablaze with lights. The launch pulled up beside a small platform; a flight of steps led up to the deck from there.

Rose went first, then Hallam, then the still-surly Bert. At the top of the stairs, a man in blue ship's uniform tried to hide his surprise at the sight of Hallam, coming aboard in buckskins.

As the three of them reached the deck, Bert tapped Hallam on the shoulder. "No guns on board, mac," he grated. "Boss's rules."

Hallam turned with a mild look on his face. "Sure," he said. He took the Colt from the holster and handed it over to Bert. "Nothin' in it but blanks, anyway."

Bert tapped him on the arm. "The pigsticker, too, Buffalo Bill."

"Bert..." Rose said in a soft, warning tone.

"Don't go nowhere 'thout my Bowie, son," Hallam answered. "And them's *my* rules."

Bert growled and squared his shoulders, but Rose cut in. "Let it go, Bert. You and Mr. Hallam have danced enough already today."

Bert let out a long breath and nodded reluctantly.

"We'll go to my private office, Hallam," Rose went on. "I can explain everything there."

"I'm ready to hear it."

The ship was crowded with drinking, gambling merrymakers from Los Angeles, and Hallam got several startled looks as he followed Rose through the main rooms to a large, opulently furnished office somewhere in the bowels of the ship. To judge from the thick carpet on the floor and the dark wood paneling, they might as well have been in a high-class office building in the city.

Rose shut the door, leaving Bert outside. Another man was waiting in the office, and he said, "Hi, Tony," as Rose went behind a huge mahogany desk and sat down.

"Art, this is Lucas Hallam, the man I told you about. Hallam, meet Art Burlington, my right-hand man."

Hallam shook hands with Burlington, who was a little taller than Rose, with dark curly hair and a pleasant, open face. "I'm glad to meet you, Mr. Hallam," he said. "I've been learning quite a bit about you."

"How's that?" Hallam asked.

"I had Art do some checking up on you before I ever approached you, Hallam," Rose said. He gestured for Hallam to take the chair in front of the big desk. "I like to know a little about someone before I offer him a job."

"Good policy. What'd you find out?"

Rose glanced at Burlington. "Art?"

"Well... your name is Lucas Hallam, and you had quite a reputation as a gunfighter in Texas and New Mexico during the Nineties," Burlington began. "Later, right after the turn of the century, you became a lawman and worked as a Federal marshal, as well as serving as sheriff of several different counties. You were also a Pinkerton agent later, and that led to you opening your own detective agency, a one-man agency, I might add, a few years ago. You also work from time to time as, ah, an actor in Western pictures. Is all that correct, Mr. Hallam?"

"Right enough," Hallam admitted.

"So you're not the simple cowboy you pretend to be." Rose said. "Which is why I want to hire you. I need a sharp operator, Hallam, and you're the guy."

"What's the job?" Some of the twang was gone from Hallam's voice now. Not all of it, though. He could emphasize the accent at will, but he could never lose it completely.

Rose leaned forward and clasped his hands together on the polished desktop. "I've been cursed," he said, "and I think you can help me put a stop to it."

A smile twitched at Hallam's wide mouth. "Don't see as how I can help you there."

Rose shook his head. "You don't understand. I've had this curse put on me—" He broke off, took a deep breath. "What I really want you to do is find the girl."

"What girl?"

"Her name is Carmen Delgado. She worked for me here on the ship as a hostess, but she was more than that. She and I were... well, you understand, Hallam."

He nodded. "Sure. And she took off on you?"

"That's right." A look of pain crossed Rose's smooth face.

"So where does the curse come in?"

"From *Mamacita*." Rose's fist banged the desk. "Damn that crazy old lady!" He stood up abruptly, went to a portable bar that was set up in one corner. He poured a drink and downed it, then said shakily, "You tell him the rest of it, Art."

Burlington took up the story. He seemed a bit embarrassed to be relating his boss's personal troubles, but he did as Rose ordered. "Carmen's mother thinks she's a witch. She and Tony don't get along, you see, never did, and when Carmen vanished her mother blamed Tony. So... so she put a curse on him."

Rose spun around. "She says I'm going to waste away and die unless she gets her little girl back!" he exclaimed. "Hell, I don't know where Carmen is. I want her back just as much as her mama does."

Hallam looked from Rose to Burlington and back to Rose. "You don't believe this old lady really is a witch, do you?"

"Of course not," Rose said uncertainly. "I don't want the old bat causing more trouble for me, though. She came out here a few nights ago, got one of her fisherman cousins to ferry her out, and raised holy hell. Yelling that I was a demon and that I stole her daughter from her. I thought I was going to have to tell Bert to throw her in the drink before she'd leave!"

"So Tony decided that the best way to placate Mrs. Delgado was to hire someone to find Carmen and bring her home." Burlington put in.

"How'd you decide on me?" Hallam asked.

Rose shrugged. "I've got friends on the force in LA, that's no secret. I asked around. They told me you were smart and honest... and stubborn. Will you take the job, Hallam?"

The room was quiet for a long moment as Hallam thought. Then he said, "Happen I do find her and she doesn't want to come back. What then?"

Rose rubbed his eyes wearily. "Then you've got to convince her mama that she's all right. I want Carmen, sure, but what I really want is for that old lady to leave me alone."

Hallam stood up, held out his hand to Rose. "I'll take the job," he said.

Rose shook hands with him, gratitude plain on his face. "I'm glad. You'll find that I'm a generous man to work for, too, Hallam. There's just one more thing. I'd like for Art to go along with you."

Hallam glanced over at Burlington. "I like to work alone."

"Art's my right hand, like I told you, Hallam. We go back a long way, and I want him to be in on this investigation, so he can keep me informed."

Hallam grimaced, thought for a minute, finally nodded his head. "We'll give it a try," he said. He put his hat on. "Come on, Mr. Burlington. I aim to go right to work on this, and I've got to change clothes first."

"Why?" Rose asked. "I think you look great in that outfit! Better than Ken Maynard, even."

Hallam squinted at him. "It may be all right for Hollywood or some floatin' saloon like this here *Gilded Lily*, but I sure as hell ain't wearin' this get-up in the real world!"

———

"MIGHT BE a good thing you're along," Hallam said to Burlington. "You can tell me where this Delgado gal lives, can't you?"

"Of course." Burlington gave Hallam the address, and Hallam pointed the roadster in the right direction.

They had taken a cab from the dock to the little house in the hills where Hallam lived. He had changed into casual clothes, but somehow he still looked like a cowboy. Night had completely fallen by now, and Hallam's roadster was only a small part of a steady stream of traffic on the gaudy streets.

"You think Carmen's room is the place to start?"

"It's *a* place to start. Might get lucky."

The rooming house where Carmen Delgado lived was on the fringes of Hollywood, in a neighborhood that had sprung up along with the rest of the town a few years before. Hallam found a parking place close to the three-story frame structure. The two men crossed a neat lawn and went up four steps onto a porch that ran the full length of the front of the house.

The door was unlocked. Hallam pushed it open. They stepped into a good-sized entrance hall.

Burlington pointed at a flight of stairs on the other side of the hall.

"No landlady?" Hallam asked.

"No need to disturb her just yet," Burlington said, holding up a set of keys. Hallam nodded, headed for the stairs.

Carmen's room was on the third floor. They didn't encounter anyone else while climbing the stairs. Hallam waited until the other man was sliding a key into the lock before asking, "Those Rose's keys?"

"No, they're mine," Burlington said. "Tony has a set, too, of course. I've had to come over here quite a few times and pick up things for Carmen when she was staying overnight on the ship. You know what I mean."

"Yep. I know what you mean."

Burlington stepped back and let Hallam enter the room first. His big hand felt around near the door, found a light switch, flipped it up. A dim bulb in an overhead fixture glowed into life.

Hallam stopped just inside the door. His boots sank into soft carpet. He grunted in surprise. "Room wasn't furnished like this when the gal rented it, I'd say."

"Tony helped her... redecorate it."

"Looks like something out of a Dodge City whorehouse."

The carpet was a rich wine-red, and so were the draperies that were hung on the walls. A long white sofa was the main piece of furniture. A huge gilt-frame mirror took up most of one wall. Hallam's assessment of the room was on target, all right.

"The bedroom's right through that door," Burlington indicated.

"Don't know if I'm up to that," Hallam rumbled. "Not after this place."

The bedroom proved to be functional and spartanly furnished, though. Looked like Carmen Delgado did her entertaining in the front room.

Hallam started working, opening the drawers in the dresser, looking in the closet, all the little tasks that made up the main part of his job. Nothing appeared to be disturbed; it looked like all the girls clothes were there, though Hallam wouldn't have known if anything was missing. Burlington confirmed his suspicion that nothing was untoward.

"The place looks like she just stepped down to the corner for something," Burlington said. "That's what's so puzzling. If it had been torn up, we would have suspected foul play."

"The girl's been missing almost a week, right?" Burlington had told Hallam the details during the trip in from the *Gilded Lily*, and now he nodded in confirmation of the big detective's question. "You and Rose been here checkin' on her since then, haven't you?"

"We both came over here to look for her," Burlington replied. "Tony has a place not far from here, so it was easy for us to drop in and see if Carmen had come back."

"You didn't bother anything here, neither of you?"

"We didn't touch a thing. Tony was worried right away, when Carmen didn't show up for work last Saturday night. We came over here then, and he told me to leave everything alone." Burlington sighed sympathetically as he thought of his boss's upset condition. "I think he was scared even then that something might have happened to her. He knew he'd have to call somebody in on the case if she didn't turn up, and he wanted all the evidence left alone."

"You talked to the landlady yet?"

Burlington nodded, then shrugged. "She doesn't know a thing. Claims she hasn't seen Carmen since a couple of days before she disappeared. The rent's paid up through the end of the month, so the old woman doesn't really care, if you ask me."

"Want to talk to her anyway."

"Sure. I'm ready if you are."

They went into the hall, Burlington locking the door behind them. As they started toward the stairs, the door of another room they were passing opened and a young woman stepped out. Her eyes got big as she swung around and saw Hallam.

"You're somebody!" she exclaimed.

"Yes, ma'am," Hallam nodded. "Lucas Hallam."

"No, I know you. You're... you're Black Tom Slade! I thought Hoot Gibson knocked you off that cliff!"

"Well, ma'am, I reckon he did." A smile played around Hallam's mouth. "That Hoot's a fine feller. I never should've gone up agin 'im."

"You certainly shouldn't have," the young woman said. "And trying to steal those poor people's range like that! You should be ashamed."

"Yes, ma'am, I am. Powerful ashamed."

Hallam hung his head, and the woman laughed gaily. "Thank you, Mr. Hallam. Lucas Hallam, was it? You knew I was just joking, didn't you?"

"Well... I figured as much."

She extended her hand. "I'm an actress, too. Sharron Devlin."

Hallam shook hands with her. "Glad to meet you.

Miss Devlin." Out of the corner of his eye, he saw Burlington fidgeting. Burlington had been impatient throughout the whole conversation, in fact.

Sharron Devlin was about twenty years old, with chestnut hair, a quick, bright smile, and a slim figure. That was enough to make any man pause for a moment, even an old cowboy.

And besides, she lived next door to Carmen Delgado.

"Were you and your friend looking for someone, Mr. Hallam?"

"Matter of fact, we were, ma'am. And call me Lucas."

"All right, Lucas. Maybe I can help you."

Hallam pointed to the door down the hall. "Hope so. We were looking for the young lady who lives there next to you."

"Carmen?" Sharron Devlin shook her head. "I haven't seen her in several days. It's been almost a week, in fact."

"Do you remember the last time you did see her?" Hallam prodded.

She frowned prettily. "I think so... I believe it was last Saturday night."

Hallam didn't look at Burlington, but he sensed the other man's sudden interest. "Saturday night, you say?"

"Yes. Yes, I'm sure of it now. I was going out, and Carmen was leaving at the same time."

"By herself?"

"Oh, no. Her date was with her." Sharron smiled, revealing dazzling white teeth. "I said hello. You know how it is with actresses, always trying to meet a producer."

"She was with a producer?"

"Well, I don't know for sure that he was a producer. But he looked like the type. You could tell he had plenty of money, anyway. His clothes were a little loud, but he didn't care. That attitude says money to me. And he was pale, real pale, like he spends a lot of time in screening rooms." Sharron shook her head. "Carmen didn't introduce me to him, though, so I guess little Sharron's unlucky again. Funny, I didn't know Carmen even wanted to be an actress."

For the first time, Burlington joined the conversation. "This man Carmen was with, was he wearing a bow tie?" His voice sounded taut, strained.

"Come to think of it, he was. Do you know him? Is he a producer?"

Burlington shook his head. "No. No, I don't know him."

"Oh." Sharron tried to hide her disappointment. She smiled again. "I've got to run, you know, important things to do. It was very nice meeting you, Mr. Hallam. Maybe we'll work together on a picture someday."

"Would be nice, ma'am. Good evenin'." Hallam would have touched his forefinger to the brim of his hat, if he had been wearing one.

Sharron Devlin hurried down the hall and disappeared around the corner of the landing. Hallam looked at Burlington and said in a low voice, "You recognized that description, didn't you?"

"I know of a guy who's pale and wears loud clothes and a bow tie," Burlington replied with a frown. "But I don't like to think about Carmen being mixed up with him."

"Who?" Hallam demanded.

"His name's Freddy Malone. He's—"

"I know who he is," Hallam cut in. "He's in the same business your boss is. Has a gambling ship, too, if I recollect right."

"You do," Burlington said grimly. "I've got a bad feeling about this, Hallam. Like the only ones with any chance of finding Carmen Delgado are the fishes."

"That's the *Astriel*," Burlington said an hour later. "That's Malone's ship."

They were sitting on a padded bench beside the railing of another motor launch. Bootleg liquor was flowing freely among the other passengers, many of them clad in tuxedos and evening gowns. Money would flow freely tonight, as well, once this group of big spenders and plungers boarded the *Astriel*.

"Will Malone's men recognize you?" Hallam asked in low tones as sea spray misted around them.

"I don't know," Burlington said bluntly. "They might. But there's going to be trouble sooner or later, whether they know me or not." His voice was dangerously soft.

"Like to make it later, if we could. After we've had a chance to ask Malone some questions."

"We'll get our chance. And Malone will tell the truth, if he knows what's good for him."

Hallam watched Burlington's face, saw the tension beneath the mask-like impassiveness. There had to be more to Anthony Rose than just another bootlegger and gambler, to inspire the kind of loyalty Hallam was seeing in Burlington.

Both men had donned hats and overcoats, but the broad-brimmed Panama only made Hallam more distinctive. With his size, though, there was no point in trying to disguise him. Malone's men didn't know *him*, at any rate, so there was no worry on that score.

"Wish I'd brought my Colt," he muttered under his breath.

Burlington heard and shook his head. "They search everybody coming on board. Nobody's heeled except Malone and his men. The guy's paranoid."

"Rose does the same thing, don't he?"

"Well, sure, but he has to, the way Malone likes to cause trouble."

Hallam didn't respond to that except to nod slowly. No point in talking about some things.

The *Astriel* was about the same size as Rose's *Gilded Lily* and every bit as flamboyant and brightly lit. Hallam felt his nerves prickling as he and Burlington boarded the ship along with the launch's other passengers, but there was no problem. Evidently, Burlington wasn't as well known as they had feared.

The casino was full and doing a booming business. Smoke and laughter and the clatter of dice and roulette wheels filled the air, along with the occasional heart-felt curse. Hallam and Burlington moved into the center of things.

"You know where the office is?" Hallam asked, pitching his voice low enough that only Burlington could hear him over the babble.

"No, but I know how to find out." Burlington pressed something into Hallam's hand. "Try to buy into a game with that."

Hallam nodded and turned away from Burlington. He made his way to a poker table, the crowd parting around his big frame. As he stopped beside the table, he dropped the thousand dollar bill that Burlington had given him onto the green baize.

"That get me into this game?"

The dealer, a slim-fingered man with a white tuxedo jacket and sleek black hair, looked at the bill for a long moment and then smiled up at Hallam. "Of course, sir. I'll have your chips brought to you." He reached for the bill.

Hallam's hand came down on the thousand before the dealer could pick it up. "I go where my money goes," Hallam said.

The dealer's professional smile never wavered. "Certainly." He snapped his fingers and a short, broad-shouldered man appeared from the crowd. "This gentleman wants some chips, Max. Kindly escort him."

The man nodded and turned away. Hallam fell in behind him. The man glanced over his shoulder and asked, "How many chips, sir?"

Hallam held up the bill. "This many, son."

"Right this way."

Hallam knew that Burlington was watching and would be close behind. The broad-shouldered man led him across the room to a closed, unobtrusive door. He opened it and stepped back to let Hallam precede him. "Right down this hall, sir. Knock on the far door."

Hallam nodded and entered the hall. He saw the door at the far end of the corridor. It was simple and unmarked, but he had a feeling that Freddy Malone was on the other side.

His long legs carried him quickly down the hall. He knocked like he had been told, and a voice from inside said. "It's open."

Hallam glanced back down the hall before he

opened the door. The first door was still ajar, but Burlington was nowhere to be seen. Hallam took a deep breath, grasped the knob and turned.

Inside, behind a metal desk piled high with paperwork, a man in flashy clothes sat and punched an adding machine. He had crisp brown hair, very pale skin, and a bow tie around his neck, he looked up at Hallam. "You want to buy chips?" he asked.

"Nope." Hallam slowly shook his head. He opened his fingers to let the thousand dollar bill float down to rest on top of the desk. "I want to pass this worthless piece of paper off on you, friend."

Freddy Malone smiled. "You're a cool one, aren't you. fella." Knew all the time my dealer had spotted the queer right off."

"They were sellin' chips outside, lots more than just a thousand. Knew I was goin' to see the boss instead. You *are* the boss, I reckon?"

"You know it, cowboy. I'm Malone. I run this ship. Now. you're leaving, and I'd like for it to be peaceful, okay?"

"Sure." Hallam paused, then said, "Soon as you tell me where Carmen Delgado is."

Malone's palms went down flat and tight against the desktop. "Rose sent you." he snarled, his lips curling. "That bastard! Trying to cover up... If anybody knows where Carmen is, it's him!" He came out of his chair, his whole body shaking with anger. "If he did anything to her, I swear I'll—"

"You'll what, you slimy little snake?" Burlington barked from the door, behind Hallam. Hallam threw him a glance, just enough to see that his clothes were rumpled and that blood was oozing from a scratch on his chin.

"Have any trouble?" Hallam asked shortly.

"Not enough to worry about," Burlington said. "Your goons need to practice more often. Freddy."

Malone shook a finger at him. "I know you! You're Rose's yes-man. Well, you can take a message back to Rose for me. He's through, you understand? Through!" Malone's voice rose shrilly, and his finger came down on a button on the desk.

Hallam sighed. Wouldn't be much time now until things got busy. His hand shot out. The fingers wrapped themselves in the front of Malone's silk shirt, lifted the little man right off his feet.

"Where's Carmen Delgado?" Hallam asked. "You were seen leavin' her place with her last Saturday, and nobody's seen her since. Might just have to take you back and give you to Rose, happen you don't decide to talk."

Malone swatted ineffectually at Hallam's arm. "You're gonna swim ashore!" he howled.

"Hallam..." Burlington suddenly said, and his voice carried a warning. Hallam kept his grip on Malone, even when he heard the ominous clicking behind him.

"Shoot the son-of-a-bitch!" Malone ordered.

Hallam looked behind him. Burlington stood with arms raised while three of Malone's men covered the room with pistols. Hallam grinned.

"You can shoot me, boys," he said, "but them popguns won't put me down in time to stop me from twistin' this feller's head right off his shoulders. Fine with me, if you're sure that's what you want."

Nobody said anything for a long moment, then

Malone gulped and said, "Back off, you fools! Can't you see the crazy old cowboy means it?"

"Damn straight I do." Hallam stepped away from the desk, and Malone came with him, still dangling from that iron grip. Hallam's arm didn't even tremble as it supported the other man's weight.

"Maybe Malone should go with us as far as the launch," Burlington suggested, lowering his hands now that Hallam was in control... at least for the moment.

"Durn good idea," Hallam agreed. "Come on, Malone."

Malone's men fell back. They had no choice. Malone's feet brushed the floor every so often as Hallam carried him out through the casino. The crowd of gamblers was stunned by the sight. The room fell silent for a few seconds as Hallam marched through, Burlington right behind him, then exploded into sound as the little procession reached the deck.

Guns were trained on the three of them all the way down the steps to the platform beside which the launch bobbed, but none of Malone's men dared make a move. When they reached the bottom, Hallam asked, "Can you run this here boat?"

"You bet," Burlington said.

"Fire 'er up. You get on out, sonny," Hallam added to the regular pilot of the launch.

When Burlington had the launch ready to go, Hallam looked at Malone. "I reckon you can swim."

Malone nodded as best he could.

"Good."

Hallam threw him into the ocean.

Guns started to crack even before Malone splashed into the dark water. Hallam threw himself into the launch as Burlington hit the throttle and sent it leaping away from the side of the ship. He heard the familiar flat *whap!* of bullets passing close by his ear, but none of them found their mark in the darkness. Burlington had the launch running flat out, and in less than a minute, they were reaching the outer limits of pistol range.

Hallam got to his feet and joined Burlington at the controls. The smaller man was gulping down lungsful of air in reaction to the tension and danger. "I thought we were dead men," he said.

"Should've knowed better," Hallam told him over the roar of the engine, "I've faced down worse bunches than that in my time."

Burlington glanced at the big man beside him. Hallam's face was calm.

"I'll bet you have," Burlington said. "I'll just bet you have."

"Well, we didn't do much good, did we?" Burlington said as Hallam stopped the roadster in front of an expensive apartment hotel. Rose had rooms there, as well as sumptuous quarters on the *Gilded Lily*. Burlington had told Hallam that the gambler would be waiting for their first report.

"Don't know as I'd say that," Hallam replied. "We found the connection between Malone and the Delgado gal, and we put the fear o' God in Malone. Maybe something'll come of it."

"I hope so," Burlington said as he got out onto the sidewalk. Hallam got out and came around the front of the roadster to join him. They started for the entrance together. The main building of the hotel was set back off the road, behind carefully tended lawns and hedges. A flagstone path led to the glass doors of the entrance

Electric lamps set in wrought iron fixtures atop poles lighted the way at intervals.

The doors of the building opened and a woman came out. She walked quickly down the path, head turned away from Hallam and Burlington. Burlington paused as she passed them, then stopped and looked over his shoulder at her. There was a thoughtful expression on his face.

"That woman sure looked familiar..."he murmured, then his eyes abruptly widened in recognition. "Grab her, Hallam!" he snapped. "That's Carmen's mother!"

The woman heard, threw a frightened glance at them, and started to run. Hallam saw a middle-aged woman with olive skin, dark eyes, and fine features, not at all the type who looked like she would be tied up with gamblers and rum-runners. *She* wasn't, of course, but her daughter definitely was.

Hallam broke into a run behind her. "Here now. ma'am!" he called. "Hold up there! We just want to talk to you."

The woman ran faster.

"I'll check on Tony!" Burlington rapped as he started to run toward the entrance. Hallam paid him no mind as he hurried after the fleeing Mrs. Delgado. Chasing down some lady wasn't really his idea of detective work, but if Burlington wanted her caught...

His long legs would have closed the gap between them in a hurry if Mrs. Delgado hadn't reached the curb and the car that was parked there. She dove into the vehicle and hit the starter. Hallam heard the growl of the engine catching and bit back a curse.

He stopped as the car pulled away from the curb with a screech of rubber. He'd never been that much of a runner to start with; nobody who'd spent over half his life in a saddle was. Now there was no chance of catching her. He drew a long breath and turned back to the apartment hotel.

There was no sign of Burlington. He had to be inside, in Rose's apartment. Hallam slapped the doors open and strode inside, then paused and looked around the opulent lobby. There was a clerk behind a desk in the corner. His face was wide-eyed and startled.

"Lookin' for Rose," Hallam told him. "Where do I find him?"

The clerk pointed at a broad staircase on the other side of the room. "Second floor," he said nervously. "Mr. Burlington just went tearing up there a few minutes ago. What's going on here?"

"That's what I want to know, friend."

Hallam took the stairs two at a time with ease. When he reached the second floor, he looked down the plushly carpeted hall just in time to see Burlington come out of one of the doors. There was a slight stagger in his step, and his face was pale and stunned.

Hallam took two steps and grabbed his shoulders. "What is it?" he asked urgently.

"Ambulance," Burlington muttered. "... need an ambulance... and the police!"

Hallam pushed him aside and went to the door of the room where Burlington had emerged. He stopped and looked inside, his face tightening until it looked like a mask of tanned, cured leather.

Anthony Rose was on his back, sprawled on the floor in the unmistakable attitude of death. One hand was flung out to the side; the other was clasped loosely around the hilt of the knife that was buried in his chest, as if he had tried to pull it out before it killed him.

Hallam heard the rasp of Burlington's breathing beside him. "That old lady always hated Tony," Burlington said. "Claimed he was a bad influence on her innocent little daughter. It looks like she gave up on witchcraft and used a more direct method to get rid of him. Damn. Damn it all!"

"Best call the police," Hallam said heavily. "There a telephone here?"

"Downstairs," Burlington answered, still staring distractedly at the body of his friend and employer. "She made sure the curse worked, didn't she? One way or another, she made sure that Tony died."

Hallam nodded. He put a big hand on Burlington's arm and pulled him away. Burlington came along without resistance, numb from his discovery.

Hallam shut the door of the room behind them.

———

"WHAT THE HELL!... Oh, it's you, Mr. Hallam." The night watchman gulped and passed a hand over his face. "You gave me quite a scare. I mean, I thought I was alone on the lot, and then I saw you... Well, no offense, but you're pretty big, and I thought you were a burglar."

"Nope, just an old cowboy," Hallam told him with a smile. "Sorry I threw a scare into you, George."

"That's all right." The watchman's face was puzzled in the pale glow from his flashlight. "Say, what're you doing here, if you don't mind my asking, Mr. Hallam?"

"Just doin' a little ruminatin', George. For some

reason, I seem to think a little better in these surroundin's. Hope you don't mind."

"Go right ahead." The watchman's voice dipped. "Between you and me, you're not supposed to be here at night, nobody is, but hell. If you can't trust a man like Lucas Hallam, who can you trust?"

Hallam clapped the little man's uniformed shoulder. "Thanks, George. Them words mean a lot to me."

"Just don't stay too long, okay? I got my job to think of, after all."

"Don't you worry none," Hallam assured him. "I'll just think through a couple of things, then head on out of here."

"Right. Good night, Mr. Hallam."

Hallam watched the man leave the saloon set, then put his back to the bar and rested his elbows on the polished hardwood surface. This was one of his favorite places, all right. Maybe it was all a fake, but it was the closest thing to his past that he had been able to find. Bill Hart had filmed part of *Hell's Hinges* here a few years before; Hallam had played one of the outlaws that Hart ran out of town. The room had been filled with smoke and noise that day as guns crashed and boomed.

He remembered other saloons and other days, when the gunsmoke had been real, when shots exploded and bullets sang and men lived and died by them. Old days...

Hallam forced his mind back to the present. Less than twelve hours had passed since Anthony Rose had appeared out on the location to hire him, but a great deal had happened during that time. Hallam went over all of it, replaying it in his mind like a director would replay a picture that he was editing. Certain things stood out. You looked at them one way and they meant something. You looked at them another way, and they meant something entirely different.

Hallam straightened. His hand went under his jacket and came out with several deadly pounds of metal. A stray beam of moonlight filtered into the saloon set and glinted off the long barrel of the Colt. Hallam spun the cylinder, checked the loads.

Then he reholstered the gun, strode to the batwings, and pushed through them, like he had hundreds of times in the past, both make-believe... and real.

This wasn't make-believe. This was a showdown. A real live showdown.

HE TOOK the regular launch out to the *Gilded Lily*, glad to be able to sit for a while and let the cool sea breeze blow in his face. Despite his determination to see this through to the finish, he was tired. The cops had kept them at Rose's apartment for quite a while, going over every facet of the story that he and Burlington had to tell. The clerk from downstairs had confirmed that Mrs. Delgado had gone up to see Rose just a few minutes before Hallam and Burlington arrived. Other tenants on the floor had revealed that they had heard angry shouting from Rose's apartment.

The police had sent out a bulletin on Mrs. Delgado. As far as they were concerned, the case would be all but closed when she was picked up.

Hallam thought different.

The guards on the *Gilded Lily* remembered him

from earlier in the evening, but when he said he wanted to see Burlington, they shook their heads. "The boss said he don't want to be disturbed," one of them told him. "Lots of things to do, you know how it is."

"Yep, I do," Hallam replied. "I still want to see Burlington, though."

The big figure of Bert, Rose's driver, bulked out of the darkness. "Having trouble, guys?" he asked.

The two guards at the top of the stairs from the launch platform shook their heads. "No problem, Bert," one of them said. "Mr. Hallam wanted to see the boss, but I told him he'll have to come back another time."

"'Fraid I've got to go in now," Hallam said flatly. He started to take a step around the guards.

"Bastard!" Bert spat as he charged forward. "You're goin' for a swim!" He swung a looping punch at Hallam's head.

Hallam moved a couple of inches to the side and let the blow whistle by his ear. He stepped in, snapped two quick punches to Bert's belly. Bert started to double over in surprise and pain.

Hallam brought up an arm like a tree branch and slammed it down on the back of Bert's neck. Bert went flat out on the deck, his face crashing into the deck with a soggy thud.

Out of the corner of his eye, Hallam saw the two guards reaching under their coats. Faster than most people could follow, his hand found the butt of the Colt and brought it out, the heavy gun behaving now like an extension of his arm, like an integral part of him. The barrel lined and the hammer clicked back before either man could finish his draw.

"Just be still, boys," Hallam said quietly. "I got no

wish to sling lead with you, happen I can get out of it. Toss them guns overboard—slow!"

The guards did as Hallam told them.

He glanced at the activity in the casino, visible through the portholes along the side of the big room. No one seemed to have noticed the short fracas outside, and Hallam had hung back deliberately until all the passengers that had been on the launch with him had entered the casino.

"I figure there's another way to get to the office, besides goin' through the gamblin' rooms. You boys better take me there, right now."

"We can't do that—"

The man broke off and gulped as the black mouth of Hallam's Colt swung his way.

"I'm gettin' on to bein' an old man, son. Don't know how many years I've got left. Reckon it's few enough that I can do a little gamblin' with them. You understand what I'm sayin'?"

The guard nodded. "I understand. We'd better do like he says, Phil."

"Yeah," the second man agreed. "I think we should."

They were agreeing too easily, even in the face of the .45. Hallam motioned for them to get started, and waited for whatever trick they had in mind.

There was another way to the office, through a series of connecting passages that avoided the big gambling room. The three of them didn't encounter anyone else, and then Hallam saw the familiar door to what had been Rose's office.

One of the guards dove toward the door, obviously intending to warn Burlington, while the other spun to jump at Hallam.

Hallam grabbed his assailant's coat with his left hand and threw him to the side, hard into the wall of the corridor. A long step brought him within reach of the other one. His arm lashed out, and the Colt slapped into the back of the man's head. He went down.

Hallam didn't waste any time. He stepped over the fallen man, opened the door of the office, stepped through and kicked it shut behind him.

"Howdy, Burlington," he said as he leveled the Colt at the two people behind the desk. "You'd be Miss Delgado, I reckon. Glad to finally meet you, ma'am."

Burlington came halfway out of his chair in surprise. His hand instinctively started to reach for one of the desk drawers, but he stopped the motion when he saw the coldness in Hallam's eyes.

The woman remained calm. No more than twenty, there was something about her that seemed much older. Her long hair, parted in the middle, was a glossy midnight black. It framed a face of classic beauty, of smooth olive skin and flashing eyes that she had inherited from her mother. Carmen Delgado was lovely. Even Hallam had to admit that...

Lovely enough to drive a man to kill for her.

"And you must be Mr. Hallam. Arthur has told me about you," she said. "You seem to be a remarkable man."

"No, ma'am," Hallam said. "But I try to be an honest one." There was an open ledger book on the desk in front of Burlington. Hallam gestured at it with his free hand and said, "Shove that over here."

Burlington hesitated, his gaze intent on Hallam as he tried to gauge the big man. Then, with a shrug, he pushed the ledger across the desk.

Hallam stepped close enough to get a good look at it, but he kept out of grabbing range. Even upside down, he was able to tell what was recorded there.

"That'd be Malone's writin' there, wouldn't it?" he asked.

Carmen smiled. "Perceptive of you, Mr. Hallam. Yes, that book is dear Freddy's private business journal. It's enough to put him out of business, if not in jail, if the authorities should get their hands on it."

"Which same is just what'll happen if he doesn't turn over the operation to you and Burlington here, isn't it? You must be hell on wheels, ma'am, pardon the expression, to get close enough to Malone in a week to weasel that out of him."

"More than a week," Carmen said in reply to Hallam's accusation. "I've been working on him for nearly a month, off and on. Freddy's a hard man to convince, but... I have ways."

"I'll just bet you do," Hallam said under his breath. "You even got Burlington to kill his boss for you, so that the two of you could take over the whole shootin' match."

"What the hell are you talking about?" Burlington exclaimed. "You saw Carmen's mother running away from there. You heard what the other tenants said about her and Tony fighting."

"Worked out real convenient for you, didn't it? Got to give you . credit for grabbin' your opportunity, Burlington. You had a witness—me—and a ready-made scapegoat, Carmen's mama. But if it hadn't happened that way, you'd've found another time and place."

Burlington's lip curled. "You can't prove any of that.

You may call yourself a detective, but you're just a cowboy actor, Hallam! Nobody's going to listen to you."

""Well, now," Hallam said. "You may be right. But if I shoot you right now, Carmen's goin' to be left 'thout anybody to look after her. She can take Malone's records back to him and tell him that you dreamed up the whole scheme and made her take a part. Malone would believe her, you can bet on that. She can lay Rose's murder at your feet, too, and get her mama off the hook for it. Not that she really cares about her mama; hell, anybody can see that."

Carmen was watching him with a mixture of hate and speculation in her dark eyes. "You have no business talking about my mother," she spat, "but the rest of what you say, it makes sense."

"Carmen!" Burlington blurted. "Don't pay any attention to this old coot!"

"This old coot's got the gun," Hallam reminded him. "You can always turn yourself in, Burlington. That, or I start blowin' holes in you."

Hallam didn't know if he would pull the trigger or not. He'd never shot an unarmed man yet, but he didn't like being used. Never had...

The explosion slammed into the ship, tilted it crazily, threw Hallam off his feet. He landed hard on the floor.

None of them knew what was happening, but like Hallam had said, Burlington knew how to seize an opportunity. His hand darted to the desk and came up with a little pistol.

Hallam saw the threat and reacted instinctively. The barrel of the Colt tipped up, and he squeezed the trigger without even thinking about it.

Burlington didn't get a shot off.

The big slug caught him in the chest and threw him backward. He was dead before he bounced off the wall behind the desk.

Carmen Delgado screamed. Hallam came to his feet, grabbed her arm, and pulled her into the corridor. The two guards he had knocked out were regaining consciousness now. Hallam paused long enough to tap them with the Colt and send them sprawling again, then headed for the outside.

At least he hoped he was heading for the deck. This maze of corridors inside the ship was more confusing than a prairie dog town.

Men in suits, carrying guns, appeared in front of him. They didn't fire, maybe because Carmen was with him and they recognized her. One of them ran up with a strained look on his face.

"Where the hell have you been, Carmen?" he snapped. "The boss was going crazy worrying about... I mean, before what happened tonight... Hell, we ain't got time to worry about that. You and the cowboy better get out of here!"

"What's goin' on?" Hallam demanded. "Maybe I can help."

The man eyed the big gun in Hallam's fist. "Maybe you can, Tex. Malone and his guys are attacking the ship. They damn near blew a hole in the bow with some kind of floating bomb. It's war, looks like." The man hefted the machine gun he was carrying. "Where's Art?" he asked Carmen.

Hallam squeezed her arm and answered for her. "We left him in the office."

The man nodded and waved the others in his party on. "I'll go get him. Why don't you two come with me?"

Hallam nodded. "Sure." He held back long enough for the others to round a corner and get out of sight, then rapped the man on top of the head with the Colt. He folded up, just like the others who had received similar treatment.

Carmen Delgado looked stunned now, stunned by the sudden violence she had witnessed in the last few minutes. Hallam turned to her and asked, "Where do they steer this thing?"

She didn't answer. Hallam put his free hand on her shoulder and shook her.

"I need to know, gal," he said urgently. "Where's the bridge, or whatever they call it?"

"I... I'll take you there," she said in so soft a voice that Hallam could barely hear her.

She was true to her word, though. With Hallam right behind her, she found her way up a couple of short staircases and onto the bridge. Two of the ship's officers were there, and they spun around as Hallam and the girl came in.

Guns were cracking all over the ship now, as a full-fledged battle continued between Malone and his men and the crew of the *Gilded Lily*. They weren't Rose's men anymore, Hallam thought, or Burlington's either, though they probably didn't know that yet. The two officers on the bridge each had a pistol on his hip, but the holster flaps were buttoned.

They wouldn't have had a chance anyway.

Hallam's Colt came up. His thumb eared back the hammer. "Where's land?" he barked.

One of the officers pointed a shaking finger off into the night.

"Well, head off that-a-way," Hallam ordered. He swung the muzzle of the Colt from one to the other to reinforce the command.

"It'll take time..." one of them said.

"Then you'd best get started."

A few minutes later, the *Gilded Lily* was underway.

"How did you know?" Carmen asked, her voice still showing her surprise and shock. "How could you possibly have known?"

"That you and Burlington were in it together? Hell, gal, I've been around a long time, remember? I saw the same thing happen in Tascosa, then later again in Santa Fe. Any time you've got two fellers goin' up against one another, you've got more folks in the background willin' to take advantage of em."

"I did nothing," she declared. "It was all Burlington's idea. He killed Anthony, he bragged to me of it."

"Glad to hear it. And I'm sure these two fellers will testify that they heard you say that. No point in your mama bein' in trouble for something she didn't do."

"No," Carmen murmured. "No point..."

The firing was more sporadic now. One side or the other, Hallam had no idea which, was winning. He heard a sudden clatter of footsteps on the stairs leading to the bridge, and he swung around to greet the newcomers.

Freddy Malone, disheveled and dripping blood from a scratch on his face, burst onto the bridge with a gun in his hand. His wild eyes fell on the girl, and he cried, "Carmen!"

She tore out of Hallam's grip and ran to the

gambler, throwing herself into his arms. "Freddy! Oh, Freddy, it was awful! *Madre Dios!*"

Malone looked over her shoulder as she buried her face against his thin chest. His face contorted. "The cowboy!" he snarled. "I figured you'd be here. I knew Rose had stolen Carmen, the bastard! Where is he? Where's Rose?"

"Figgered that's why you started this little fracas," Hallam said grimly. "Well, you're a mite late—"

"He killed Rose and Burlington!" Carmen cried as she huddled against Malone. "He's trying to take over, Freddy—"

Then she was turning, a smaller gun appearing in her hand from some hiding place in her clothes. Malone, too, was lining his sights on Hallam.

Hallam triggered off four shots before either Malone or Carmen could fire. The rolling thunder sent Carmen's pistol spinning from her fingers, cylinder shattered. Malone went spinning away as the other three bullets ripped into him

The silence that fell over the bridge was as awful as the fury that had preceded it.

The first sound was Carmen's sobs as she clutched her nerve-deadened hand. Then Hallam heard the sirens and became aware of the searchlights playing over the ship. He smiled as he realized that his plan had worked. The *Gilded Lily* was inside the limit now, and the Coast Guard, always interested in the gambling ships that sailed up and down off the coast, was converging.

Hallam holstered his Colt. There would be all kinds of questions from the authorities and he might even hear some threats about lifting his license from the

District Attorney. Hell, it had been a lot simpler in the old days. Then he could have gotten onto his horse and ridden off into the sunset, like Hoot and Colonel Tim and all the others did now.

That was progress for you.

When it was over, though, he thought he might look up that little actress—Sharron Devlin, that was her name—and chew the fat with her. She had struck him as the type who liked to listen.

There were still some people who liked to hear about the good old days...

THE BLUE BURRO

In "The Blue Burro", Hallam's search for a kidnapping victim leads him to a shady bordertown nightclub and plunges him into a deadly tangle of international intrigue with high stakes.

THE NIGHT BEFORE, Hallam had said, "The Blue Burro is the sort of place a fella with enough money can buy anything his heart desires... 'cept maybe an honest drink."

Tonight, before his eyes, that assessment had been borne out. He'd been sitting at a table in a corner of the smoky cantina for a couple of hours, nursing a succession of watered-down drinks, and during that time he had watched the ownership of stolen jewelry, packages of dope, and underage girls change hands a dozen times or more. Most of what he saw filled him with anger and the desire to haul out the hogleg under his coat and let daylight through the innards of the skunks responsible for it.

But he was here to do a favor for an old friend, a friend who had once saved his life, and until that job was done, Hallam had to rein in his temper.

Besides, Race had hinted that there was a lot riding on this assignment, a whole hell of a lot. Things that maybe affected the whole blamed country...

———

BOTH MEN HAD WORN the star-in-a-circle badge when they rode together in South Texas, hunting outlaws in the brush country along the border. Jim Race had been a sergeant in the Texas Rangers, and so had Lucas Hallam. Eventually, Hallam had left the force and hired on with the Pinkertons, but Race had stayed in the Rangers and made captain. More than fifteen years had passed. Roads were paved now, and automobiles chugged and clattered along them. Nary a horse was tied up in front of buildings lit up by electricity. Over in Europe, nation fought against nation using metal behemoths that lumbered along through bloody mud and flimsy contraptions of wood and canvas that soared overhead through smoke-filled skies. Everything had changed in the world.

But when Hallam got the telegram from Jim Race asking him for help, Hallam had come without hesitation. Some things, it seemed, did not change.

They met in a room in the Camino Real Hotel, in downtown El Paso. When Hallam opened the door and saw Race standing there, memories came rushing in on him.

The two of them pinned down in a shack on the banks of the Nueces River, their horses dead... Hallam with a bullet in his leg, unable to run... standing off rush after rush of the outlaws who wanted to kill them, until night finally fell... the way Jim Race had hoisted the much larger Hallam over a shoulder and gone out the back of the shack under cover of darkness, carrying him across the river and a couple of miles to an isolated ranch where they had gotten help...

It had been a heck of a thing to do, especially since Hallam had urged Race to slip out alone after dark. He would stay there, he had said, and keep the gang busy until Race was long gone. Race hadn't even considered the idea. He'd grinned and said, "You wouldn't do that if the tables were turned, now would you, Lucas?"

Hallam hadn't been able to say honestly that he would have, and so that was that.

Now as they faced each other in the hotel room, Race took off his hat—a fedora, for God's sake, not a Stetson!—revealing a lot of gray in his reddish hair. He stuck out a hand and said, "Lucas, it's mighty good to see you again."

Hallam shook with him and looked at the brown tweed suit. "I thought you was still a Ranger."

"I am. Captain, in fact. Reckon you could say I'm undercover."

Hallam grunted.

"Too many people in El Paso know me," Race went on. "This get-up's not going to fool anybody for very long, but at least I won't draw as much attention to myself dressed this way. I don't want anybody to know about you and me talking."

Hallam nodded. During his time as a Pinkerton operative, he'd had clients who needed to keep everything between them secret. This wasn't really the same thing, but in a way it was. If he took the job, whatever it was, he wouldn't get paid, but he'd be working for the Texas Rangers anyway.

"I got a bottle and some glasses. Sit down and tell me about the trouble you got."

Race laughed humorlessly. "You mean a fella can't want to get together with an old trail partner without having anything else in mind?"

"That telegram sounded to me like you needed a hand with something," Hallam said as he splashed whiskey into the pair of glasses on the night stand. He handed one to Race, took the other himself. "You want to drink to old times?"

"Hell, no," Race said. "Mostly they weren't near as good as we remember 'em."

"Probably not."

"I'll drink to the future instead."

Hallam shrugged and clinked his glass against Race's. "To the future."

"Let's hope there is one."

Now that was a damned odd thing to say, Hallam thought. He tossed back the hooch, licked his lips. "Tell me about it," he said again.

Without being asked, Race sat down on the edge of the bed and put the fedora on the spread beside him. "I'm looking for a fella named Kenneth Langham. He's supposed to be somewhere over in Juarez."

"Young fella?"

"Twenty-three."

Hallam nodded. Young Americans went missing in Juarez all too often. Most of them stumbled back over the river bridge sooner or later, once they got their fill of whatever fleshpot or dope den that had swallowed them up for a while. Some of them landed in jail on the wrong side of the border, and that was just too bad. A good number wound up dead, and that was worse, but still, there wasn't a whole hell of a lot you could do about it. Somebody bound and determined to wreck their life would usually find a way to do it.

"I didn't think the Rangers handled missing persons cases."

"Young Langham's father has money."

"Oh," Hallam said, but that still didn't really explain anything. In his experience, the Rangers didn't do favors for rich men. But he had been away for a while. Maybe that was something else that had changed.

"Normally, all we'd do is contact the authorities in Juarez and let them look into it," Race went on. "You know how much good that would do, though."

"More than likely not much," Hallam said.

Race nodded. "And we can't operate across the border ourselves." He smiled faintly. "It's not like the old days, Lucas, when jurisdictional lines could be... bent a mite every now and then. Relations between the U.S. and Mexico are especially strained right now, what with Carranza taking over and Villa raising such a ruckus all over the place and nobody much knowing who's going to be in power from one day to the next..." Race shook his head.

"So what you need," Hallam said, "is for somebody who's a civilian to go over the river and look for Langham."

Race looked squarely at him and said, "Yes. That's exactly what we need."

"Got any idea where to start lookin'?"

That was when Race had said, "Have you ever heard of a cantina and gambling den called the Blue Burro?"

———

THE BLUE BURRO was owned by a man named Gonsalves, who also owned a ranch a dozen miles or so below the border. Hallam had heard plenty about him but had never met the man. Most of what Hallam had heard was bad. Gonsalves was said to have personally killed at least eight men and ordered the deaths of many more. In the old days he would have been a bandido. Now he was just a businessman who was somewhat more ruthless than normal.

"Good luck, Lucas," Jim Race had said the night before when he left the hotel room. "And thanks. There's a lot riding on this. More than I can say. Walter Langham is a mighty important man. Important to the whole country."

The name had been a little familiar to Hallam. He had gone to the El Paso Public Library during the day and read some newspapers. Walter Langham was Langham Steel. He could probably get away with calling President Wilson "Woody" if he wanted to. How in blazes had the son of a man like that gotten mixed up with a polecat like Rico Gonsalves? Then he remembered all the other rich men's sons who had gotten themselves in trouble. Yeah, there was always a way. And Race had been pretty positive about the tip the Rangers had gotten that Kenneth Langham was spending a lot of time at the Blue Burro, one of Cuidad Juarez's most notorious dives.

Being a civilian, Hallam could grab the kid, drag him across the river to El Paso, and turn him over to the Rangers, who could then ship him back to his daddy. Of course, if Kenneth raised a big enough ruckus before Hallam got him out of Juarez, the Mexican police might arrest him for kidnapping, and he'd probably never see the light of day again. Hallam would do his best to see that that didn't happen.

"Señor, por favor? You like a girl, señor? You like me?"

Hallam turned his head and looked up and saw a girl standing there at his shoulder. She was a dark-haired, dark-eyed beauty, no doubt about that, but Hallam figured she wasn't over sixteen. She rested a hand with long red fingernails on his shoulder and leaned over so that he could get a good look down the low neck of her blouse.

"No thanks, honey," Hallam told her, feeling even older than his forty-four years. He wished he could tell her to get out of this hellhole, but he knew that even if he did, it wouldn't do any good.

She leaned even closer, breathing into his ear in English, "I think they're going to try to kill you soon."

Hallam wasn't expecting that. She hadn't sounded Mexican at all when she said it, and as he glanced at her again he decided that despite the dark hair and eyes and the olive skin, she was American. And maybe a mite older than he had first thought, too.

"Who?"

"The two at the bar... there... I heard them talking about you. They work for Gonsalves."

Hallam looked where the girl indicated with a flick of

her eyes. Two men stood with their backs to the bar, watching the room. Hallam had already pegged them as a couple of Gonsalves' enforcers. One was Mexican and about as wide as he was tall. The other one had pale hair cropped short and a face like a wedge. His eyes were pale, too, and they lit on the table where Hallam was sitting.

The girl leaned in still more, twined an arm around Hallam's neck, and kissed him. She put a lot of feeling into it. She sure as hell didn't kiss like a sixteen-year-old, Hallam thought, and then reminded himself that it had been a long time since he had kissed a gal that age. He didn't really know how a sixteen-year-old would kiss in these modern times.

"Who are you?" he asked between his teeth when she pulled away.

"Just somebody trying to do a fellow American a favor. I think you'd better get out of here while you still can, mister."

"They're watchin' me. If they want to kill me, they won't just let me leave."

She reached down and took his hand. "Come with me. I know a way out."

Hallam's mind worked fast. This might be a trap. Assuming that the fellas at the bar really did want to kill him, the girl could be working with them, trying to lure him someplace where they could dispose of him without too much fuss. Or she could be telling the truth about wanting to help him. Of course, that left unanswered the question of why an American girl was pretending to be a whore in a Juarez cantina.

If he played along, he might find out, Hallam decided.

He held the girl's hand as he came to his feet. "Lead the way," he said.

She tugged him toward an arched doorway with a beaded curtain over it. Hallam had seen girls taking customers through here all evening, so there shouldn't be anything suspicious about what they were doing. The girl glanced back at him and said quietly, "They're still watching. I don't like the way they're talking to each other. I think they've realized that I'm not one of the regular girls."

"Best not waste any time, then."

The beads rattled as they pushed through them. The hall on the other side was lit only by a few candles stuck here and there. It was narrow, with a lot of doors on both sides and a door at the far end. The girl let go of Hallam's hand and hurried toward that door.

"It'll be locked," she said over her shoulder. "Can you break it down, or pick the lock?"

"Comes down to it, I'll shoot it open."

She looked at him again. "You've got a gun?"

"Yep."

"Good. You may need it."

One of the doors on the left side of the hall opened. A heavyset American stepped out, grinning back into the tiny room at the girl who sat nude on the bed, counting the money he had left her. "You did fine for your first time, darlin', just fine," the man told her. Hallam bumped him hard with a shoulder as he went past. "Hey!"

The beads rattled loudly.

"Get back in there," Hallam said.

"Who the hell do you think you are, bud?"

Hallam thought about leaving him there in the line

of fire—anybody dumb enough to think he'd found himself a virgin in the back room of a bordertown cantina was pretty close to being too stupid to live—but instead he put a hand on the man's meaty shoulder and gave him a hard shove that sent him flying back onto the bed. The nude girl jumped out of the way.

"Go!" Hallam said to the girl in front of him.

She ran the last ten feet to the door at the end of the hall. Hallam was right behind her. He reached under his coat and drew the .45 revolver from the holster canted on his left hip. Somebody yelled, "Alto!" but didn't wait to see if he was going to stop. A gun roared, the sound deafening in the narrow confines of the hallway.

The bullet spanked past Hallam and gouged a big hole in the cheap plaster on the wall. He twisted, saw the two men who'd been at the bar coming after them. It was the pale-haired man who had fired; smoke drifted from the barrel of the gun in his hand. His Mexican compadre had a knife with a long, heavy blade. The thing was damn near a machete. There wasn't much room to do it, but Hallam put a bullet between them that made them jump in opposite directions and run into the walls.

"Get out of the way," he said to the girl as he turned back toward her.

She huddled in a corner as he launched himself against the door. It was sturdier than it looked, but Hallam was a big man and knew how to hit a door. The wood around the lock splintered.

Hallam stumbled a little as he went through the door, but he was still able to reach back with his left hand, grab the girl's arm, and drag her after him. Two more shots blasted. Hallam flung the girl down the alley toward a distant spot of light and then dropped to one knee. Since he always carried the hammer on an empty chamber, he had four rounds left in the Colt. He slammed all four of them down the hall, hoping none of the whores or their customers would pick that moment to step out.

The pale-haired man went down, clawing at a bullet-torn thigh. The Mexican pitched forward, too, but Hallam sensed that he wasn't hit, just getting out of the way of the lead. Hallam got to his feet, feeling a twinge in his bad knee as he pushed up, and then he ran after the girl. His boots splashed through muck in the alley, and he thought he stepped on a rat or two.

"Over here," she called as he reached the mouth of the alley. She was behind the wheel of a Model T with the top pushed back. Hallam ran over and cranked the engine while she held down the starter. The engine caught.

"You know how to drive this thing?" Hallam asked over the coughing and sputtering.

"Just get in!"

Hallam used his long legs to step over the passenger side door without opening it. He dropped onto the seat as the automobile lurched forward. He put the Colt back in its holster and then hung on.

In the lights from the buildings they passed, he saw her grinning at him. "First time in an auto, cowboy?"

"No," Hallam said. He frowned as the contraption swerved around a corner. "I'm just not real fond of 'em, that's all."

"Well, we'd better hope Gonsalves' boys don't have one handy, or they'll come after us."

"The gringo won't. I put a forty-five through his leg."

"Good for you."

There were fewer automobiles over here in Juarez than across the river in El Paso. At this time of night, Hallam and the girl pretty much had the streets to themselves. She drove past the big downtown mercado, which was closed, and stopped in a small park. The place was deserted.

"I'm obliged for your help," Hallam said.

"Why did Gonsalves' men want to kill you?"

"Don't know. Why did you decide to give me a hand?"

"I couldn't stand by and let a fellow American be murdered."

"That's another thing," Hallam said. "What was an American girl doin' at the Blue Burro?"

She laughed. "A girl has to make a living somehow—"

"No," Hallam said, "you ain't a whore. Who are you, lady?"

"I'm the one who helped you, remember? I don't think you have a right to ask questions."

Hallam opened the door of the Model T. "All right, then, I reckon I'll be movin' on."

She hesitated, but only for a second, before saying, "Wait. Please."

Hallam had figured from the first that she wanted something from him. He had no idea what it might be, but she would either tell him now or he would walk away. He had business of his own over here, and it meant that he would probably have to venture back to the Blue Burro before this night was over.

He sat there with the door half open and waited in silence. After a moment, the girl said, "My name is Jacqueline Southwick."

"Fancy name."

"This is where you're supposed to ask if I'm one of the Philadelphia Southwicks."

"I reckon you must be," Hallam said, "or else you wouldn't've brought it up."

"Yes, I am. I came down here to look for someone. A... a young man."

"Your beau?"

"That's right. At least... I thought he cared about me. Now I'm not so sure. He... he abandoned me on a trip through Texas, while we were in Dallas. I should have gone home, I know... I could have wired my father for a train ticket... but I was afraid something was wrong, that my friend might be in trouble. I heard he was in El Paso, so I came out here. I had enough money for that. Then I heard that he had been seen in Juarez, at a place called the Blue Burro, so I dressed myself like the sort of... the sort of woman who would frequent such a place, and I came to look for him."

Hallam thought about the story. It was just oddball enough to be true, but he wasn't sure yet if he believed her.

"You're rich?" he asked.

"Well... my family is. My money is actually in a trust fund that I can't touch until I'm twenty-one. That's still two years from now."

"And you ran off on a lark with a young fella and came to Texas. Did the two of you elope?"

She shook her head. "No, we're not married. I know, it's positively scandalous—"

Hallam held up a hand to stop her. "But the whole adventure got fouled up when the young fella dumped you in Dallas, and you're a mite too ashamed to go slinkin' back home to your folks."

Her chin lifted angrily. "If you have to be so crude about it, I suppose that's a reasonable assessment."

"How long have you been hangin' around the Blue Burro lookin' for the young fella?"

"This is the third night."

"You been posin' as a soiled dove for three nights and ain't had to..."

"Young women of my class are quite adept at promising more than they ever intend to deliver," she said.

Hallam just shook his head. Jacqueline Southwick had no idea how lucky she had been. He was going to have to see to it that she took herself back across the river and stayed there. He didn't need that headache on top of his job for the Rangers, but he couldn't just leave her to wolves like Gonsalves and his boys, either. She thought of herself as an adventuress, but really she was just a lamb waiting to be gobbled up.

"You didn't ever find your beau, did you?"

"No. But I think I know where he is. I overheard Gonsalves talking to some of his men." She leaned toward Hallam, excited and animated as she spoke. "I think they took Kenneth down to Gonsalves' ranch."

"Kenneth?" Hallam said.

"Yes, that's my friend's name. Kenneth Langham. Of the Pittsburgh Langhams."

Hallam was still digesting that when she grabbed his arm and said, "The minute I saw you, I knew you were the man to help me. Will you take me to

Gonsalves' ranch and help me rescue Kenneth? I know that awful man is holding him prisoner! He probably intends to demand some sort of ransom from Kenneth's father."

That sounded likely to Hallam, if indeed it was true that Kenneth Langham was at Gonsalves' ranch. Having Jacqueline Southwick fall into his lap, so to speak, had filled in some of the blanks for Hallam. Even without meeting Langham, Hallam had him pegged as a wild young man, too full of himself for his own good, the sort who would drag a gal halfway across the country and then desert her and run off to gamble and whore his way into trouble on the wrong side of the border. Easy pickin's for a man like Gonsalves, who was always in the market for a fast, dirty dollar. Langham probably never expected his girlfriend to try to track him down, and he probably hadn't figured that his father would use the influence of power and money to set the Rangers looking for him, either. Those strands had intertwined and brought Hallam and Jacqueline together.

Had Jim Race known about the girl? Hallam doubted it. Race would have warned him about that possible complication. And even though she had given him a hand, she was a complication, one that he didn't need.

"Maybe I'll go and look for your fella," Hallam said, "but you got to get back across the river to El Paso."

"Oh, no," she said instantly. "I'm going with you, Mister—What is your name, anyway?"

"Lucas Hallam, and if I'm goin' to pluck your beau away from Gonsalves, I can't be lookin' out for you at the same time, Miss Southwick."

"You won't have to look out for me. I can take care of myself. In fact, I helped you get away, back at the Blue Burro, remember?"

"And I said that I'm obliged—"

"Besides, if I go along we can take my car, and we can be at Gonsalves' ranch before morning. I have a pretty good idea of how to get there. If you go alone, you'll have to either walk or find a horse, and it'll take you a lot longer."

Hallam tried not to sigh in frustration. "You don't know what you're gettin' into—"

"I can shoot if I have to." Her hand dipped into the folds of the long skirt she wore, and from somewhere she came up with a small pistol. It gleamed in the faint light that penetrated the shadows under the trees. "Just give me a chance, Mr. Hallam. I... I have to help Kenneth if I can."

Hallam knew it was the wrong thing to do. He knew he ought to take her across the river by force if necessary and make her stay there. But once he was gone, how could he stop her from following him? If she was bound and determined to be part of this, maybe it would better to keep her close by, rather than having her blunder around and maybe cause even more problems.

Besides, there in the rear hallway of the Blue Burro, she had seemed pretty cool-headed. She drove the automobile good, too, he thought. Better than he could, that was for damned sure. And if they succeeded in snatching Kenneth Langham away from Gonsalves, they would need to rattle their hocks out of there in a hurry.

"All right," he said, hoping that he wouldn't regret

it. "You can come with me. But you got to do what I tell you to do."

"Of course." He couldn't really see her face in the shadows, but he could hear the smile in her voice as she added, "Should we seal the bargain with another kiss?"

"Just drive," Hallam told her.

———

HALLAM HAD A PRETTY good idea where Gonsalves' ranch was, and Jacqueline had overheard enough to confirm the location. They found the main road leading south out of Juarez and followed it.

Hallam thought about what had happened at the Blue Burro. Why had Gonsalves' thugs come after him? They shouldn't have known who he was, and they sure shouldn't have had any idea that he was there on a job for the Texas Rangers. And yet the girl had overheard them plotting to kill him, and they had come after him as soon as he'd made a move to get away. Had someone found out about his meeting with Jim Race and put two and two together? An even more disturbing question occurred to Hallam. Did Gonsalves have an informer working inside the Rangers?

He would worry about that once he had rescued Kenneth Langham, Hallam told himself. He felt a stirring of resentment. Not only was he risking his own life on the young man's behalf, but a beautiful young woman like Jacqueline was putting herself in danger because of him. It sounded to Hallam like Kenneth Langham needed to grow up a whole heap. Somebody ought to shake some sense into his head. Maybe, if he had the chance, he would give the boy a good talking to.

Not that it would accomplish much, more than likely. Youngsters like that thought they had the world by the tail, just because their fathers had money. They might grow old, but they seldom grew up.

Kenneth Langham would at least have the chance, if Hallam had anything to say about it.

———

JACQUELINE TALKED QUITE A BIT, raising her voice over the rattle of the engine. She complained about the way her folks treated her, always prodding her to do things she didn't want to do and telling her she couldn't do the things she really wanted to. Hallam figured out pretty quick that she was a smart girl, smart enough so that a life of sitting around drinking tea and going to society parties bored the hell out of her.

"I think I'd like to learn how to pilot an aeroplane," she said. "Don't you think that would be fun, Mr. Hallam?"

Hallam had seen a few of those flying machines, and they bothered him more than automobiles did. "I reckon I'll stay on the ground," he said. "I never wanted to be higher up than the back of a good horse."

"Oh, pooh. You're a spoilsport, just like my father. He thought it was completely improper for me to learn how to drive. Young ladies just don't do such things, according to him."

"Well, maybe they shouldn't."

"Despite your rough exterior, you're just like him. I can tell that now."

That was the first time anybody had ever told

Hallam that he was just like some rich man from Philadelphia.

"I'm going to learn how to pilot an aeroplane," Jacqueline went on, "and someday I'm going to fly off in one and visit all the jungles and deserts in the world and have all sorts of thrilling adventures. And if my father doesn't like it, that's just too bad. I'll be a grown woman soon, and I'll do what I want."

Hallam hoped she lived through this night, so that she would have a chance to be a grown woman. It hadn't seemed to occur to her that she was in the middle of one of those thrilling adventures right now.

That was because it didn't seem so thrilling while it was going on, Hallam mused. When your life was actually in danger, everything seemed a mite confusing and frightening, and usually you had to be both lucky and good to survive. Especially lucky.

"Of course, once Kenneth and I are married, he'll probably try to tell me what to do, too," Jacqueline went on. "But will I listen to him?"

"Probably not," Hallam said.

She laughed. "That's right. Probably not!"

The road was rough, and the ride shook up Hallam's insides more than any horseback ride he had ever taken. The Model T rattled so much he didn't see how it held together. But somehow it did, and along about three in the morning, they came to the side road that led to Gonsalves' ranch. Jacqueline turned west, toward a range of low hills. Hallam saw the faint twinkle of lights a couple of miles away. That would be the ranch.

The sound of the automobile's engine would carry quite a ways in the night air. When they came to a small gully with gently sloping sides, Hallam said, "Drive down in there, over behind that clump of mesquite. We'll go the rest of the way on foot."

"We're not going to drive all the way to the ranch?"

"Not unless you want them to know we're comin'."

"Oh. Yes, that makes sense. We'll hide the auto here and come back for it once Kenneth is with us." She drove down into the wash.

Hallam didn't intend to walk back here. He figured they could get their hands on some horses, there on Gonsalves' ranch, and ride back to the automobile. If need be, they could just forget about the contraption and horseback all the way to the border. Wouldn't be the first time he had ridden across the Rio Grande that way, Hallam thought with a faint smile. Wouldn't even be the first time he had crossed the border with some-body chasing him.

"I don't reckon there's any chance I could talk you into stayin' here and waitin' for me?"

"Of course not."

Hallam gave some thought to tying her up and making her wait here. But he knew she'd put up a fight, and more importantly, if anything happened so that he couldn't get back to the automobile, then she really would be in a fix. Like it or not, he was stuck with her. In a way, he had been ever since she had sidled up to him in the Blue Burro.

"Come on," he said.

His boots had low heels, so walking wasn't too bad a chore. Jacqueline wore slippers, though, and they didn't give her feet much protection from the rocks and gravel on the road. She didn't complain, but she couldn't help but say "Ouch!" from time to time. Hallam was glad they didn't have that awful far to go.

They were about halfway to the lights that marked the ranch when he heard something. He stopped and turned and looked to the south. Another automobile was coming up the main road from that direction. Its headlights cast yellow cones in the darkness. Those beams of lights bounced up and down as the automobile hit rough spots.

Hallam figured the vehicle would go on past the ranch trail, but the lights slowed and then swung to the west. "Somebody's comin'," he said. "Get off the trail."

Jacqueline didn't argue. She hustled off into the scrubby brush with Hallam following her. "Squat down," he told her when they were about fifty yards off the road.

"I don't believe anyone has ever told me to squat before. That's another of those things proper young ladies of Philadelphia society don't do."

"We're a hell of a long way from Philadelphia," Hallam said. He hunkered on his heels and waited with the Colt in his hand.

There was enough moonlight and starlight for him to be able to see the automobile as it approached. It wasn't a Model T, he saw. This contraption was some-what bigger and heavier. He leaned toward Jacqueline and asked, "You know what kind of automobile that is?"

"I think it's a Mercedes-Benz touring car." She sounded puzzled. "That's a German automobile. I wouldn't expect to find one down here."

The Mercedes-Benz, if that's what it was, rumbled on past the spot where they waited. "Well, it looks like it's goin' to Gonsalves' ranch, just like us." Hallam waited until the red lights on the back of the automobile had vanished, then stood and motioned for her to follow him.

They resumed walking toward the ranch. Hallam didn't holster the Colt, and he noticed that Jacqueline had the little pistol in her hand, as well. "You sure you can shoot that thing?"

"I'm an excellent shot. I've been to a target range in Philadelphia several times."

"Ever shot at anybody who's shootin' at you?" Hallam asked, already knowing the answer.

"No, but if I have to, I will."

"Before the night's over, you'll probably have to."

There were a lot of lights burning at the ranch, Hallam saw as they drew closer, more than should have been at this time of night. In fact, it looked like the whole place was awake. That wasn't good. He had hoped they could slip in, locate Kenneth Langham, and get out with him before anybody noticed. Hallam figured the young man would be guarded, but he wasn't worried about taking care of a couple of guards. If he had to fight all of Gonsalves' men, though, it would be a different story.

The house had been there for a long time, a sprawling, two-story Mexican hacienda made of whitewashed adobe, with red slate tiles on its roof. There was an outer wall, also of adobe, with a black wrought-iron gate in it. The house would have an inner courtyard with a fountain in it, overlooked by a second-floor balcony that ran all the way around. Once the place had been owned by a real ranchero, a don who raised fine cattle and horses, instead of a whoremonger and dope smuggler like Gonsalves. Hallam wondered how Gonsalves had gotten his filthy hands on the ranch. It was probably an ugly story.

The big German touring automobile was parked in front of the gate. A man wearing some sort of uniform leaned against the front fender, smoking a cigarette. That would be the driver, Hallam thought. Another man strolled over from the gate. He wore a town suit and a peaked sombrero. One of Gonsalves' guards. Hallam and Jacqueline watched the two men for a moment as they crouched behind some brush, then Hallam whispered, "Give me a few minutes to work my way around closer to them, then you walk up bold as brass."

"I'm going to distract them while you attack them, is that right?"

"I reckon that's the general idea," Hallam said. "You up to it?"

"Of course!"

He squeezed her shoulder for a second, then moved off into the darkness, circling closer to the wall so he could come up behind the two men. For a big man, he moved with a quiet grace that made his passage through the shadows nearly soundless. He wound up kneeling beside the adobe wall about a dozen feet from the driver and the guard. They didn't have any idea he was there.

Hallam had been waiting only a moment when Jacqueline strolled into the light and approached the automobile. "Hello, boys," she said in a sweet, lilting voice. Both men turned sharply to stare at her, startled to see anyone come walking out of the night, let alone a beautiful young woman. Out of habit, they reached under their coats, and Hallam knew they were reaching for guns.

He was on them before they knew what happened. His big hands closed on their heads and smashed their skulls together with a sound like a watermelon being dropped on the floor. The two men collapsed without any chance to raise an alarm. Hallam didn't think either of them would wake up for quite a while.

Jacqueline ran lightly over to him. "Did you kill them?" she whispered, sounding a little awestruck.

"They ain't dead... I don't think," Hallam told her. He took her arm. "Come on."

The gate was half-open. They slipped through. Hallam led the way along the wall of the hacienda until they reached a corner where a stairway led up to the second floor. As quietly as possible, they climbed the steps, went through a narrow passage, and found themselves on the balcony overlooking the interior courtyard. A railing of black wrought-iron that matched the exterior gate ran along the edge of the balcony. The fountain down in the courtyard laughed and gurgled, and a man laughed, too. It wasn't nearly as pretty a sound.

Hallam catfooted along the balcony toward the voices he heard. Jacqueline followed him, and he certainly couldn't complain about her making too much noise. She was as quiet as an Apache.

The trees growing around the fountain had lanterns in them. Hallam and Jacqueline stayed well back so that the light from the lanterns didn't reach them. It spilled over the two men who sat in comfortable chairs beside the fountain, though. Hallam recognized Gonsalves, a slender, narrow-faced man with a mustache. The other man was shorter and thicker, with close-cropped gray hair and one of those monocle things stuck in his eye. He wore an expensive suit and toyed with a heavy walking stick made from some sort of gnarled wood.

"When the time comes, you will have my country's gratitude officially, Señor Gonsalves," the gray-haired man said. "Until then, you have my gratitude, unofficially, for your assistance in this matter."

"It was my pleasure, Excellency," Gonsalves said. "You will speak to the Kaiser on my behalf?"

"Most assuredly."

Hallam frowned. The Kaiser? That was the fella who was the big boss over in Germany, and the gray-haired man in the courtyard below looked and sounded German, as far as Hallam could tell, not being an expert on such things. Why was somebody who worked for the Kaiser paying a visit to a cheap Mexican crook like Gonsalves?

And where was Kenneth Langham?

"Will the young man be here shortly?" the gray-haired man asked. "It is a long journey back to Mexico City, and I wish to delay it as little as possible."

"I sent one of my men to wake him," Gonsalves said. "He should be here soon."

A door opened somewhere down below. Footsteps rang on the flagstones that paved the courtyard. A voice said, "Herr Rammelman, it's good to see you."

Jacqueline's fingers dug into Hallam's arm. "That's Kenneth," she hissed.

Hallam had already figured as much. And as Kenneth Langham strolled up to join Gonsalves and the German, it was obvious that he wasn't a prisoner after all. He wore a lounging jacket, and a cigarette dangled from his lips. He shook hands with Rammelman.

"What's he doing?" Jacqueline hissed. "What's going on here?"

Hallam didn't know the answers, but he figured if they kept quiet, they might learn them. He put a finger to his lips and touched Jacqueline's shoulder lightly with his other hand.

Kenneth sat down with Gonsalves and Rammelman. A jug of tequila sat on a small table, along with some glasses. Kenneth poured a drink for himself. The other two men already had glasses in their hands. Kenneth lifted his glass and said, "My father sends his regards, Herr Rammelman... along with a more tangible token of his esteem."

Rammelman grunted. "More than a token, Herr Langham. Half a million dollars is a great deal of money. More than enough to persuade Señor Villa to assist us."

"Here's to war," Kenneth Langham said.

Hallam's head was spinning. Kenneth Langham hadn't been kidnapped. He had come here to Gonsalves' ranch voluntarily, and he had brought half a million dollars with him, delivering it on behalf of his father. Walter Langham had built a fortune in steel... and that fortune would only grow larger if the United States became involved in a war. But a war with who? Mexico?

The men tossed back their tequila. Gonsalves licked his lips and said, "Herr Rammelman, you must make it clear to Villa that I will be the territorial governor once he is in power. That is my fee for arranging this meeting."

"Of course," Rammelman said. He reached inside his coat and brought out a sheaf of papers. "Everything is set forth in these documents. General Villa will attack the United States and draw them into a war in their own back yard, so to speak, so that the Americans will have neither the time nor the inclination to interfere with our affairs in Europe. Then, once we have been successful, we will assist Mexico in turn to reclaim all the territory stolen from her by the Yankees. Everyone profits by this arrangement... including, of course, Herr Langham and his father."

Kenneth smiled. "The money's in my room. Why don't I go get it before Villa gets here?"

"An excellent idea," Rammelman said. He laughed. "I must admit, I am a bit curious to see what half a million American dollars looks like."

Kenneth stood up and walked under the balcony, out of sight. Hallam glanced over at Jacqueline. Her face was drawn tight, and her eyes were wide with shock and anger. He took her arm and drew her back into a darkened alcove.

"He... he's a traitor!" she whispered, her voice shaking a little from the depth of her feelings. "I thought I knew him, but I didn't know him at all!"

"Take it easy," Hallam said. "This changes everything. We got to figure out what to do."

"Oh pooh, I don't want to rescue him anymore, that's for sure! He made his own choice to join up with these... these hoodlums."

"Yeah, but if we leave him here, he's goin' to turn over half a million bucks to Pancho Villa, and Villa's goin' to try to start a war with the United States. I don't know about you, but I don't care much for that idea."

"Neither do I," Jacqueline said. "How do we stop them?"

Hallam's rugged face creased in a grin. He had hoped she would see things that way. "Come on."

They found some more stairs and hurried down to the first floor. Speed and stealth were their most important allies, Hallam thought. He looked along the covered walkway where several doors were located. Kenneth Langham had come out of one of those rooms. Beyond them, Gonsalves and Rammelman were visible sitting next to the fountain, but the two men weren't paying any attention to the shadowy corner where Hallam and Jacqueline lurked. They were still drinking and talking.

Hallam and Jacqueline peered around the corner of the adobe wall at the doors. Hallam talked in a swift whisper, and Jacqueline nodded. When one of the doors opened and Kenneth Langham stepped out carrying a small leather suitcase, Jacqueline stepped around the corner and softly called his name.

Kenneth stopped and looked, staring at her in surprise. If he yelled, they were in for a fracas, Hallam thought, but instead, the young man was so shocked to see the girl he had left behind in Dallas that he took a step toward her and said, "Jacqueline...?"

Hallam couldn't see Kenneth Langham from where he stood, but he could see Jacqueline just fine. He watched her smile and beckon to Kenneth, and as pretty as she was, dressed in that long, colorful skirt and low-cut white blouse, it would take most young men a lot of willpower to turn down that invitation. Kenneth didn't have that much willpower. He hurried along the flagstone walk, bringing the suitcase with him. Jacqueline retreated around the corner. Right about now,

Kenneth had to be wondering if he had imagined her. He had to find out.

He stepped around the corner, right into Hallam's fist.

The punch landed solidly on Kenneth's jaw, jolting his head back and making his eyes roll up in their sockets. At the same time, Hallam used his other hand to grab Kenneth's coat and keep the young man from falling. He jerked Kenneth's limp form deeper into the shadows.

"Did... did you hurt him?" Jacqueline asked as Hallam lowered Kenneth to the ground. She might claim she no longer cared for him, but some habits were hard to break.

"Just knocked him out," Hallam said. "Grab that bag."

Jacqueline picked it up. "It's heavy."

"Blood money usually is." Hallam risked another glance around the corner. Gonsalves and Rammelman were still sitting by the fountain, drinking and smoking. They didn't seem worried that Kenneth Langham hadn't returned yet.

Even though Hallam had seen only the two men he had knocked out at the gate, he figured Gonsalves had at least a dozen more men at his beck and call, and all of them would be hardened killers. It would take only a shout to summon them. The smart thing to do would be to throw Kenneth over his shoulder and get the hell out of here. He and Jacqueline could slip back to the Model T and light a shuck for Juarez. Once they made it over the border to El Paso, Hallam could dump the kid and the money in Jim Race's lap and let the Rangers sort out everything.

And yet, he couldn't help but think of those documents Rammelman had placed on the table next to the tequila. The papers detailed the whole German plot involving Pancho Villa attacking the United States. It seemed to Hallam that it would be a good thing for the American authorities to have those papers.

"Take the suitcase," he told Jacqueline. "Get back to the automobile and wait for me. If you hear a bunch of shootin', though, you better take off and get back to El Paso as fast as you can. When you get there, take the money to a Texas Ranger named Jim Race and tell him everything that happened."

"A Ranger? Are you a Ranger, Mr. Hallam?"

"Used to be. Right now I'm just givin' them a hand."

"I knew as soon as I saw you I could trust you to help me. That's why I said what I did about Gonsalves' men plotting against you."

"Wait a minute," Hallam said. "You mean they weren't talkin' about killin' me?"

"Well... no. As a matter of fact, they were after me. I thought if I pretended to help you, then you would help me."

So when the two gents had chased them down the hallway in the back of the Blue Burro, they had been trying to get their hands on Jacqueline, not him, Hallam thought. He had figured it was the other way around. It looked like just about everything in this business had turned out to be something different than it appeared to be at first glance.

"I'm sorry," Jacqueline said. "I shouldn't have lied to you."

"That's all right," Hallam said. He hadn't spilled

the whole story of his involvement to her, either. "Take the money and get out of here."

"Please... be careful. And bring Kenneth with you, if you can."

"If I can," Hallam promised.

She slipped off into the night, taking the suitcase with her, and as soon as she was gone Hallam used Kenneth's belt to tie the young man's hands behind his back. He found a handkerchief in Kenneth's pocket and crammed it in his mouth to serve as a gag. Then Hallam left him sitting there against the wall, still unconscious.

He didn't know much about those new-fangled automobiles, but he knew they ran on gasoline. When he got back to the Mercedes-Benz parked in front of the hacienda, he found the two men he had knocked out still lying slumped beside the vehicle, out of sight from the house. Hallam caught them under the arms and dragged them farther away from the automobile. Then he went back and poked around the contraption until he found the spout where gasoline was put into it. He unscrewed the cap, sniffed to make sure he had the right place, and made a face at the stink. People claimed that automobiles would eventually do away with the smell of horseshit, but as far as Hallam was concerned they weren't really much of an improvement.

He pulled the tail of his shirt out, tore some strips of cloth off it, and knotted them together. Then he lowered the makeshift fuse down into the gasoline tank, letting some of it dangle out. He waited a minute to allow the fabric to soak up some of the gasoline and then fished a match out of his pocket. He snapped it into life on his thumbnail and held the flame to the cloth. It caught fire and began to burn. The lower it went, the faster it would go.

Hallam turned and ran back toward the house.

Kenneth Langham was gone when Hallam got to the place where he had left the young man. Hallam bit back a curse and drew his gun. Kenneth must have come to and managed to get to his feet. He had stumbled off looking for help, which meant that any second—

Out in the courtyard, Gonsalves started yelling in Spanish.

A second later, the Mercedes-Benz blew up, lighting the night sky with a brilliant splash of flame.

Hallam ducked around the corner and broke into a run, heading toward the fountain. He saw Rammelman trying to untie Kenneth. Gonsalves was gone, no doubt heading for the front of the house where the explosion had just rocked the place. Kenneth saw Hallam coming and let out a yell. Rammelman spun around and jerked out a gun.

Hallam didn't see a German diplomat, didn't think about the possibility of an international incident. He just saw a fella pointing a gun at him. After that, instinct took over, and the revolver bucked in Hallam's hand as he fired.

The bullet spun Rammelman around and dropped him to the flagstones. He hunched over, badly wounded. Kenneth's hands were free now, and he made a dive for the gun Rammelman had dropped. Hallam lunged forward and kicked him before he could get it, breaking his jaw. Kenneth sprawled on the ground, knocked senseless again.

The documents still lay on the table. Hallam

scooped them up with his free hand and jammed them inside his coat. He bent, picked up Kenneth Langham, and tossed the young man over his shoulder. The boy was skinny and didn't weigh too much. Hallam headed for the back, knowing he couldn't go out the front. That was where Gonsalves and his men would be congregating, where the Mercedes-Benz still burned fiercely.

Hallam was half-right and half-wrong. Gonsalves' men might be at the front of the hacienda, but Gonsalves himself came trotting out of the rear wing, carrying a shotgun. When he saw Hallam coming toward him, he jerked the greener up and fired.

Hallam felt the bite of buckshot, but he also heard the deadly thud of lead into Kenneth Langham's body. Kenneth jerked and slipped out of Hallam's grasp as Hallam fell to one knee. The Colt came up and roared as Gonsalves tried to reload. The Mexican cried out as Hallam's bullet tore into him and drove him backward. He dropped the Greener and tumbled onto the flagstones, barely twitching when he landed.

Hallam looked at Kenneth and saw that the lounging jacket was sodden with blood, as was Hallam's coat. Most of the blood on Hallam had belonged to Kenneth. The young man had caught the brunt of the shotgun blast, and it had pretty much blown him in half, although Hallam's life had been saved in the process. Hallam hadn't meant for it to happen that way, though. He didn't hide behind any man, and sure as hell not a traitor.

Traitor or not, Jacqueline was going to be upset to hear that Kenneth was dead.

But she'd never hear about it if he didn't get away from here, Hallam told himself. He lurched to his feet, ignoring the hot, wet pain where a few of the lead pellets had ripped through his side, and ran out the back of the hacienda, kicking open a rear gate.

He circled the place and headed for the gully where he and Jacqueline had left the Model T. He hoped she was still there. The idea of walking all the way back to Juarez, shot up as he was, didn't appeal much to him.

Lights bloomed in the darkness in front of him before he got there. An engine roared and clattered. Hallam leaped aside, but the automobile skidded to a stop before it reached him. "Mr. Hallam!" Jacqueline cried.

Hallam tumbled over the side door and gasped, "Go!"

She hesitated. "Kenneth...?"

"He didn't make it," Hallam said through his teeth. The pain in his side was getting worse.

Jacqueline hesitated only an instant to let that soak in. Then she spun the wheel and tromped the foot feed. The wheels threw sand and gravel in the air as the automobile slewed around and took off. Shots banged from the hacienda, but none of the bullets came close.

Hallam figured they were about halfway to Juarez before he passed out.

————

HE WAS SITTING at the bar in the Camino Real when Jim Race slipped onto the stool beside him. The tightly wrapped bandages around Hallam's torso didn't keep him from lifting a glass of whiskey to his lips.

"Nobody can raise quite as big a ruckus as Lucas Hallam," Race said quietly. It was the middle of the afternoon and they were alone at the bar, it being siesta time for the locals.

"You sent me down there," Hallam pointed out.

"To look for a missing kid, not to uncover some German plot to start a war."

Hallam shrugged. "I found the kid."

"And he wound up dead, too."

"Gonsalves did that, not me."

"Yeah." Race signaled the bartender for a drink. When the man had brought it and gone, the Ranger went on, "Those papers had too much blood on them to be legible, you know. Kenneth Langham's blood."

"I told you what they said. And you got the half-million. That's got to be proof of something."

"Yeah, but what?" Race shook his head. "The word is, we're letting the whole thing drop. As far as the Rangers—and all the rest of the authorities on this side of the border—are concerned, we don't know a damned thing about it."

Hallam grunted. "What about Walter Langham?"

"What about him? All he knows is that his boy went into Mexico and didn't come back. A damned shame, but these things happen."

Hallam sipped his whiskey. "Why did Langham pretend to want Kenneth found in the first place?"

"It was just a formality, a report so that if anything happened to the boy, Langham would look like an innocent, concerned father. He didn't really expect us to do anything about it. That's my guess, anyway."

A hard smile touched Hallam's face. "So in a way, it was Langham's own fault that his plan got ruined and his boy got killed."

"If you want to look at it that way. Unofficially,

Langham will be investigated... but a man with that much power and money... don't expect too much justice, Lucas."

"Not too much," Hallam said, thinking about Kenneth Langham. "Just enough."

After a moment, Race said, "What about the girl? Can she be trusted to keep her mouth shut?"

"I reckon. She's pretty smart. Got me back here in one piece, didn't she? Anyway, she's goin' to be busy for a while." Hallam grinned. "She's goin' to buy herself one o' them aeroplanes and learn how to fly it. Says she wants to take me up for a spin."

"Lucas Hallam in an aeroplane?" Race snorted. "I don't believe it!"

"You never know, Jim," Hallam said. "You just never know."

———

A COUPLE OF YEARS LATER, Mexican rebel troops under the command of Pancho Villa crossed the border and raided the town of Columbus, New Mexico, killing sixteen people and prompting the United States to send a punitive expedition into Mexico after him, commanded by General John J. "Blackjack" Pershing. That failed expedition did nothing to stop the United States, and Pershing, from a year later entering what was then known as the Great War. Hallam sometimes wondered what, exactly, had prompted Villa to attack Columbus. One thing was certain: if the attack was part of a German plot, Walter Langham didn't have anything to do with it. The steel magnate had blown his own brains out three months after his son's death in Mexico. It was in all the papers.

Jacqueline Southwick learned how to fly an aeroplane, one of the first women to do so, but she didn't fly off and have any more adventures. She married a rich young fella back in Philadelphia instead. Before that, though, she spent some time in California with Hallam, and she probably would have stayed longer if he had just said the word, which he didn't. He was too old for her, whether she wanted to believe that or not.

So when it came time for her to leave, she kissed him one last time and then got on the train, and as Hallam watched it pull out of the station, he smiled and said softly to himself, "Oh, pooh."

PICTURES IN THE STARS

Pictures in the Stars finds Lucas Hallam searching for a missing astronomer in a case involving surprisingly high stakes.

HALLAM FELT as out of place as a horned toad in a ballroom.

He looked at the scientific equipment surrounding him, lifted his eyes to take in the great curving dome far above his head. A big slice was opening up in the dome, and as it widened, the lights in the place began to dim. Stars winked into view through the opening in the roof. The faint hum of electric motors came to Hallam's ears.

"I think you'll be interested in this, Mr. Hallam," the white-coated man beside him said.

Hallam didn't say anything, just nodded and fought down the vague nervousness that was gnawing at him. He was used to open spaces, and being inside a massive building like this bothered him some.

"There you are," Dr. Bauer said, bending and gazing

through the eyepiece of the great telescope. After a moment, he straightened and offered, "Take a look."

He stepped away from the telescope and Hallam took his place. Bending awkwardly, Hallam looked through the eyepiece. The stars, which should have been mere pinpricks of light, suddenly seemed to leap at him.

"What do you think?" Bauer asked.

Hallam hesitated a moment, then rumbled, "Mighty impressive." He didn't add that he preferred looking at the stars from the open range, rather than through a 100-inch telescope.

The call from Dr. Bauer asking that he drive up to the Mount Wilson Observatory near Pasadena had come as a surprise to Hallam. He wasn't sure why an astronomer wanted to talk to a private detective. He had arrived just as Bauer and his staff were getting ready to open the dome for the night's work, and Bauer had requested that Hallam wait a few minutes until things were underway. The offer to let Hallam look through the giant telescope had come on the spur of the moment.

Lucas Hallam was a big man, tall and broad-shouldered. His hands were large, and his craggy face with its long gray mustache added to his rough appearance. He wore boots and jeans and a tan-colored cotton shirt with the sleeves rolled up. He had a suit and a Panama hat that he could wear when he had to, but he hadn't expected to be working today. Bauer's call had come late in the afternoon.

Hallam wasn't going to turn down work. It had been several weeks since he had had a client, and he hadn't done any movie work since falling off a horse and twisting his knee while doing a picture with Hoot Gibson. He'd had surgery on the knee a few months earlier, and luckily it wasn't hurt bad, just enough to keep him off a horse for a while. The Hooter was a good kid and had offered to find another part in the picture for Hallam, but it would have been a nonriding job, and Hallam wanted none of that. The knee was considerably better now, though, and Tom Mix was starting a new picture the next week. Come Monday morning, Hallam would take a *pasear* down to Gower Gulch and try to pick up some work there.

That gave him four days to devote to whatever job Dr. Bauer had for him.

Hallam stepped back as one of the white-coated assistants hurried past him, bent on some errand. The young man bent and looked through the telescope, then muttered something under his breath and scribbled some numbers on a piece of paper. None of it made any sense to Hallam.

One of the other young men walked up to Dr. Bauer. He had tightly curled red hair and blue eyes that looked out intensely from his pale face. "Is this the detective?" he asked Bauer.

"I told you I would handle this, Garrett," Bauer said stiffly. "I appreciate your concern—"

"Kevin's my friend," the young man interrupted. "I want to help in any way that I can."

Clearly, Bauer was annoyed that Garrett had broken in while he was speaking. "If there is anything you can do, I will be sure to let you know," he said. "Now, if you will excuse us."

He wasn't asking for permission, but rather dismissing the young man. Garrett started to say something else, then closed his mouth and stalked away. His behavior didn't strike Hallam as a smart way to act around the fella who ran the place.

"Perhaps we should go to my office, Mr. Hallam," Bauer said.

Bauer led him to a small room on the far side of the building. In a round structure like the observatory, there weren't any corners. When Bauer flipped on a lamp on his desk, the light seemed bright after the gloom of the big main chamber.

The office was full of books and papers, but they were neatly in place for the most part. There were several maps on the walls, maps of stars that Hallam supposed represented the solar system or the galaxy or something.

Bauer sat down behind the desk and waved Hallam into a straight-backed chair on the other side. He clasped his hands together and asked, "Are you familiar with the stars, Mr. Hallam?"

"Only to find my way around by them," Hallam replied. "You ride enough back trails, you get to where you can steer by 'em."

"The stars have been my life's work. I have been the director of this observatory since its opening in 1904. That is more than twenty years of my life, and before that I studied and observed the heavens all over the world. I have even discovered a few stars and named them. Perhaps by looking up so much, however, I have lost track of what is happening down here on the ground."

Hallam said nothing, waited for him to continue.

"Well," Bauer said after a moment, making his voice more brisk, "I suppose I had better tell you why I called you, Mr. Hallam. One of my assistants here at the observatory, a young man named Kevin Jeffries, seems to have... disappeared. I would like for you to look for him."

Hallam frowned. "Most folks go to the police about a missing person."

"I know that." Bauer nodded. "But I have a feeling that Kevin would not want me to do that."

Hallam felt his curiosity perk up. "Why not?"

The astronomer looked down at his desk, then back up at Hallam. "I suppose you could say that Kevin is keeping a secret. He would not want all the publicity that would result if it was known that he was missing. I am afraid the newspapers would make quite a sensational thing of it."

Bauer fell silent again, and Hallam waited a minute before asking, "You goin' to explain that, Doctor?"

"Our conversation is confidential, correct?"

"Legally it ain't, not until you hire me, but when a man asks me to keep shut about something, I generally do it."

"Kevin's father is Thornton Jeffries."

Hallam grimaced. That simple statement explained a lot. Though he hadn't been in southern California at the time, he had heard the stories of how Thornton Jeffries had become almost an overnight millionaire when oil was found on his property years earlier. Since that time, Jeffries had done nothing but get richer. Oil, orange groves, real estate during the land booms... Thornton Jeffries had a hand in all of them.

"Didn't know Jeffries had a son," Hallam grunted.

"I do not think he is overly proud of Kevin," Bauer said with a sigh. "He had in mind that Kevin would eventually take over the family business, but Kevin had no interest in such things. He wanted to be an astronomer instead. His father never understood."

"How long's the boy been missin'?"

"Two days. Thirty-six hours, actually. He was here Tuesday night, but he did not come in yesterday or today."

Hallam leaned forward, hunching his shoulders slightly. "Reckon you're right about the newspapers," he said. "They'd have a high old time with a story like this. But you know that boy could be in bad trouble, him bein' a rich man's son and all."

Bauer sighed again, his weariness evident. "I realize that, Mr. Hallam. It is possible that he has been kidnapped or robbed or—Lord knows what might have happened to him."

"You sure he ain't just off doin' something on his own?"

"He would have told me if he could not come in," Bauer said. "He was very serious about the work we do here, not a frivolous young man like so many you see these days. Besides, he has a special project of his own that he has been working on, an important project. When he was not here Wednesday, I tried to call him and did not get an answer. The same was true today. I am very worried about him, Mr. Hallam, but I hesitated to call the police. Kevin wants to be out of his father's shadow, to make it on his own. That is why I decided to hire a private detective."

Hallam nodded slowly. "Reckon I could look into it for you," he said, coming to the decision as he spoke. "Not unless you agree to something else, though."

"I am prepared to pay any reasonable fee—"

Hallam cut him off with a wave of a big hand. "If I haven't turned the boy up by tomorrow night, I want you to report this to the police. That's the condition."

Bauer considered briefly, then nodded. "You are right, of course. But you will give the case twenty-four hours?"

Hallam nodded again and stood up. "I'll need his address and telephone number. Don't suppose you've got a picture of him?"

Bauer shook his head as he wrote on a pad of paper. He tore the slip off and handed it to Hallam. "There is his address and number. I can give you a description of Kevin. He's tall and rather thin, with dark hair that is usually parted in the middle." A slight smile touched Bauer's face. "Recently he has been attempting to grow a mustache, as well. So far, he has not been too successful."

"He got any friends that you know of?"

"That young man who was talking to me outside, Garrett Alderson, is his best friend, I suppose. They have known each other for quite some time."

"What about women?"

"Really, Mr. Hallam, how would I know? Oh, there was one young lady up here one day. Kevin was showing her the telescope." Bauer coughed discreetly. "I imagine that Garrett could tell you her name. He was here that day, too, and I gathered that he was also interested in the girl."

"What about the boy's father? You checked with him to see if he knows where his son is?"

"I called the Jeffries estate and asked if he was there. Whoever I talked to, a butler I suppose, told me that Kevin has his own house. I already knew that, of course.

The man said that Kevin had not been there for several months."

"You didn't tell anybody there that Kevin's missin'?"

Bauer shook his head.

It seemed to Hallam like the astronomer was taking an awful lot of responsibility on himself in this matter. The cops should have been notified, and the boy's family sure as hell should have been told. Those were decisions that weren't up to him, though. Bauer had made them already. Hallam's only decision was whether or not to take the case, and he had already made up his mind on that one.

"Reckon I could use your office to talk to this Garrett Alderson?"

Bauer stood up. "I will ask him to step in here."

He went out, leaving the office door open, and a few minutes later, Garrett Alderson appeared there. "Dr. Bauer said you wanted to see me, Mr...?"

"Hallam, Lucas Hallam. You and this Kevin Jeffries were friends, right?"

Alderson nodded. He said, "Kevin and I met at Stanford. We were both studying astronomy, and we used to help each other out on the work."

"You have any idea where he might've got off to?"

"None at all," Alderson replied with a shake of his head. "I think if Kevin had been planning to go away, he would have told me about it."

"The other folks who work here, do they know he's missin'?"

Alderson shrugged. "I suppose they've noticed he hasn't been at work, but as far as I know, Dr. Bauer and I are the only ones who are worried."

"Does Kevin have any other friends besides you, somebody who might know where he is?"

"He always kept to himself... No, sir, I can't think of anyone."

Hallam reached up and rubbed his jaw thoughtfully. "How about this gal who was up here, the one who was lookin' at the telescope? You know who she is?"

Alderson's eyes dropped, and he seemed uncomfortable as he answered, "Her name is Elena Fleming."

"She Kevin's girlfriend?"

"I suppose you could say that."

"But you're a little sweet on her yourself, ain't you?"

Alderson glanced up, his gaze meeting Hallam's again. "I used to go with her," he said sharply. "In fact, I introduced her to Kevin. But that was after she and I had broken up."

"Hold on, son. Didn't mean no offense. You know where the girl lives?"

"She has a house in Pasadena, not far from Kevin's place." Alderson frowned at Hallam. "Are you going to get her mixed up in this?"

"Just thought I'd ask her a few questions. She might know more of what was on the boy's mind than anybody else."

"I suppose so," Alderson said grudgingly. He gave Hallam the girl's address, then said, "Is there anything else?"

"No, I reckon that's all for now," Hallam said. "Thanks for talkin' to me."

Alderson paused in the door. "I hope you find Kevin, Mr. Hallam. He's a good friend, and I wouldn't want anything to happen to him."

"I'll give it my best shot, son."

Hallam wasn't sure how good his best shot could be in this case, though. As he pointed his flivver back down the winding road that led to the base of Mount Wilson, he thought about what he had been told so far. It wasn't much to go on, but it was enough to stir up some unpleasant speculations.

Anytime someone with a rich relative vanished, the most obvious possibility was kidnapping. Kevin Jeffries had kept his relationship to his father pretty quiet, but someone could have found out and decided that putting the snatch on the boy would be a good way to get some money out of old Thornton Jeffries.

If that was the case, there would be a ransom demand. Hallam would nose around awhile, try to turn up something on his own, but if he was unsuccessful, he would have to go to Kevin's father and find out if he had heard anything.

He had to go back through Pasadena anyway to get to Hollywood. Might as well stop by Kevin's house and take a look around, Hallam thought.

It was a small, neat bungalow on an avenue of small, neat bungalows, well-lit by streetlights. Hallam eased the flivver to the curb and stopped in front of the house Kevin Jeffries was renting. He killed the engine, waited a minute before he got out and shut the door softly.

There was light in the house, a soft glow that was there, then gone, then back again.

Looked like someone was searching the place with a candle.

Hallam reached through the open window of the car on the passenger's side and opened the glove box. Coiled up inside was an old-fashioned holster and shell belt, and inside the holster was a long-barreled Colt Peacemaker. Hallam slid the weapon from the holster and then dropped the belt back on the car seat. The smooth walnut grips of the Colt felt good against his callused palm.

He went across the yard toward the house, moving with an efficient grace unusual in a big man.

The front door was locked. Hallam went to the side of the house, moved along it silently to the back. There was a screened-in porch there. That door was unhooked, and the door leading into the kitchen was open, too.

Hallam paused just inside the house, letting his ears work, picking up small sounds that told him the intruder—the *other* intruder, he thought wryly, since he hadn't been invited in himself—was in the front part of the house. His eyes had adjusted enough to show him vague shapes where the furniture was. Hallam started through the kitchen, toward the rooms where the other person was. Suddenly, he saw the glow of the candle again, filling a doorway. He stopped in his tracks, the Colt coming up to cover the door as the glow became stronger.

The soft scrape of a shoe behind him was all the warning he had.

Hallam started to whirl, but he was just a little too late. Something hard bounced off his skull, staggering him. He lashed out with the Colt, not wanting to shoot, and caught a glimpse of a face in the dim candlelight filtering in from the other room and the glow from a streetlight coming through a side window. The blow missed, and he heard a grunt of effort as the other man swung again. This time the sap didn't hit him a glancing blow. It connected solidly, and Hallam went down as pain exploded behind his eyes. He felt the Colt slip from his fingers, but there was nothing he could do to stop it.

He didn't go under completely. He heard a man's voice rasp a curse and then the sound of running footsteps. Hallam forced himself up on hands and knees, trying to ignore the fierce pounding in his head, and started to feel around for his fallen gun.

The overhead light clicked on, blinding him, and something sharp came down painfully on his hand. He jerked back, heard a female voice exclaim, "Oh!" Then, "Don't you move! I've got a gun, and I'm not afraid to use it!"

Hallam looked up, blinking, trying to make his eyes start working again, and slowly focused on the shape standing over him.

It was a good shape, young and trim and curved in the right places, topped with an attractive face and a shower of thick brunette hair. The girl was a looker, and she was truthful, too.

There was a gun in her hand, a small revolver, and it was pointed right at Hallam's head.

"Hold on, miss," Hallam said, keeping his voice calm. He didn't like the wild look in the girl's eyes. "No call to go pointin' that hogleg at me. I mean you no harm."

"Wh-what are you doing here?"

Moving slowly so as not to spook her, Hallam drew in the hand she had just stomped with a high-heeled shoe. There was a small cut on the back of it. He said, "Reckon you'd be Elena Fleming."

She looked surprised. "How did you know that, Mr.

Hallam? And what exactly are you doing lying on the kitchen floor?"

Now it was Hallam's turn to be surprised. He asked, "Do I know you, miss? You do look a mite familiar."

Elena Fleming smiled a tight smile but didn't lower the gun. "We haven't actually worked together, but I've heard about you."

Hallam nodded, remembering suddenly that he had seen her on the set of a Doug Fairbanks picture. "You're an actress."

"Just bit parts so far, but that's going to change," she said with a positive tone. "But that doesn't explain what you're doing in Kevin's house."

The gun hadn't moved an inch during the conversation. Hallam said in an even tone, "I'm also a private detective. Actin' is just a side job for me. That Dr. Bauer feller hired me to look for Kevin Jeffries. And as for why I was lyin' on the kitchen floor, as you put it, some sneakin' snake-in-the-grass hit me on the head."

The barrel of the pistol finally sagged toward the floor as relief washed over Elena Fleming's features. "My God, I thought you were one of the kidnappers!" she exclaimed.

Hallam figured it was safe to stand up now. She was holding the gun loosely, her arm hanging at her side. He got to his feet, scooping up his own Colt and tucking it behind his belt.

"You know for sure Kevin's been kidnapped?" he asked, his voice sharp.

Elena shook her head. "But he wouldn't just disappear without telling me. We're... we're engaged to be married. We have no secrets from each other. Something unexpected—something bad—must have happened to Kevin."

"That's the way it looks to me, too, but I haven't had a chance to do much lookin' into the matter, yet. Mind tellin' me what you were doin' pokin' around his house in the dark?"

"I was checking to see if he had come back. I came over last night, after Kevin didn't call me all day, but there was no sign of him. And I've worried so much since then I had to come back over. Besides, someone has to feed his fish."

"Fish?"

"Kevin has an aquarium with tropical fish, some quite rare species, in fact," Elena said. "Would you like to see them?"

Hallam's knowledge of fish extended to hooking rainbow trout out of a high mountain stream and pan-frying them, but that was about it. "I'll take your word for that," he told her. "How'd you get in?"

Her features began to turn crimson as she blushed. "Really, Mr. Hallam... Kevin and I *are* engaged. I have a key."

Hallam reached up and carefully touched the knot on his head, wincing as pain radiated from it. "Did you see anybody when you came in tonight?"

Elena shook her head. "The house seemed empty. If there was anyone here, he was hiding from me."

"Why didn't you turn the lights on?"

Elena laughed shortly, but there was no humor in it. "You haven't met Mrs. White yet, I take it. Kevin's next-door neighbor?"

Hallam shook his head, and damned if it didn't hurt.

"She seems to think that Kevin is her son. At any rate, she treats him like he is. And she doesn't approve of me at all. I didn't want her to see a light and come over here thinking Kevin was home. Why, if she knew I had a key to his house, the poor boy would never hear the end of it. She'd tell him I was just a brazen, shameless hussy! You know how some people feel about actresses."

That made sense to Hallam. He said, "You didn't find any sign of Kevin havin' been here yesterday or today?"

"None at all."

"Are any of his things missin'? You know, like clothes and a bag?"

"I couldn't find anything at all missing. Oh, Mr. Hallam ... "Her voice cracked slightly. "I'm so worried about him."

"Don't you fret none," Hallam said, reaching out rather awkwardly to touch her shoulder. "We'll find that feller of yours, and I'm sure he'll be just fine."

"I hope so."

Hallam kept the rest of his thoughts to himself. Now that his head was a little clearer, he recalled the face of the man who had hit him. Even though he had seen the features only for a split second, something in the back of Hallam's mind had thought they were familiar. Now, in the last few minutes, he had finally dredged up the memory and put a name with the face—Myron Dart.

And Myron Dart was nothing but hired muscle, a strong-arm man for Walter Tyrone.

Who was damn near the biggest crook in Los

Angeles at the moment, if you didn't count the politicians.

Nope, Hallam thought, things didn't look too good for Kevin Jeffries, and they were getting worse by the minute.

It was a toss-up where Hallam would find Walter Tyrone. Tyrone frequented the best nightclubs in Hollywood, and there were plenty of them. After he and Elena Fleming left Kevin's house rather quickly so that Mrs. White next door wouldn't get suspicious, he sent Elena home with a promise to get in touch with her right away if he found Kevin or discovered anything about him. Then he looked in at the Cocoanut Grove and the Montmartre Cafe before getting lucky at a relatively new nightspot called the Red Top. A half-dollar got the parking lot attendant to admit that Tyrone had gone into the club earlier in the evening, in company with "one red-hot mama, lemme tell ya," as the youngster put it.

Hallam nodded, headed for the door of the club.

He expected to be stopped, and he was. The doorman, a beefy type whose shoulders strained the fabric of his gaudy red coat, put a hand on Hallam's chest and said, "You ain't goin' in there dressed like that, buddy. This ain't no cowboy saloon."

Hallam put a sorrowful look on his face and shook his head. "Mr. Tyrone's goin' to be powerful upset when he finds out you didn't let me in, pard," he said. "I got an important message for him."

"You can give me any message you got. I'll see that it gets to Mr. Tyrone."

"Nope, can't do it. This here word's got to be delivered personal-like." Hallam seemed to brighten. "Say, ol'

Myron come in just a little while ago, didn't he, sort of worked up?" Without waiting for the doorman to respond, Hallam went on quickly, "Tell him I got news about Kevin. Can you do that?"

"Sure, sure," the doorman muttered. He stepped inside for a few moments, then reappeared. "Just wait right here, buddy. Don't run off."

"Don't intend to," Hallam said.

He hooked his thumbs in his belt and stood waiting, and as he did, he looked around the nightclub's entrance. There was a curving driveway with a red canopy over it directly in front of the heavy wooden double doors. Small windows were set in each door, but they had smoked glass in them and could not be seen through. Hallam had been inside the Red Top a couple of times, though, and he knew that beyond the small foyer was a big room, sunken a couple of feet below ground level and filled with the usual tables and chairs, with a bar along one wall, booths along the other, and a bandstand and tiny dance floor at the far end. The club's primary distinguishing feature was its huge skylight of blood-red glass. Lights mounted on the roof shone down through the glass, casting a red glow that moved around the club as the motors mounted on the lights made them rotate. It was a fancy gimmick in a town noted for fancy gimmicks. The place was popular now, but once the novelty of it wore off, the stars and starmakers of Hollywood might find themselves a new watering hole.

The entrance doors slapped open abruptly, and Myron Dart strode out, a scowl on his face. He was as broad as Hallam but not quite as tall, and his bald head had ugly ridges of flesh running from above his ears around to the back of his skull. In an angry voice, he demanded, "Where's this gink lookin' for me?" then his gaze fell on Hallam and he exclaimed, "You!"

Hallam had his feet braced, and the muscles of his shoulders bunched as he brought a knobby fist up and slammed it in the middle of Dart's startled expression.

All the power of Hallam's body was behind the punch, and with a howl, Dart flew back through the swinging doors, hit the drop-off where the main room of the club stepped down, and fell flat on his back. Women started to scream. Hallam didn't pay the commotion any mind. He brushed past the doorman, who was too stunned to stop him, and strode into the Red Top.

Myron Dart was trying to get up again, and at the same time was reaching under his coat. Hallam hooked his arm with the toe of his boot, jerked it away from the butt of the gun in Dart's shoulder holster, then let his foot come down on the wrist. Dart yelped as bones crunched together.

"Don't like it when somebody uses a sap on me," Hallam told him, pressing down a little harder. "Where's your boss?"

"Right here," a voice crackled. "What the hell are you doing, mister?"

Hallam looked up to see a well-dressed, handsome man with sleek dark hair standing next to a table, his clean-cut features mottled with rage. Still seated at the table, her mouth open in shock, was one of the most beautiful women Hallam had ever seen. He recognized her right away—Gail Sumner. She'd played a few second leads, and according to the gossip Hallam heard around the lots, she was poised for bigger and better things. A big publicity push was just getting underway.

"You'd be Walter Tyrone, I reckon," Hallam said to Gail Sumner's escort. "Seen your picture in the paper a time or two."

"Who the devil are you?" Tyrone demanded.

"Name's Lucas Hallam."

"I don't know you, Mr. Hallam, but that's my personal assistant you're assaulting, and I demand that you stop it right now."

"This personal assistant of yours—" Hallam looked down at Myron Dart, who was writhing in pain. "Reckon thug'd be a better word for him... Anyway, he clouted me with a sap earlier this evenin', and I didn't take kindly to it. I want to know why he was hidin' in Kevin Jeffries' house and waitin' to hit folks on the head."

Before Tyrone could answer, Hallam heard rapid footsteps behind him. A glance over his shoulder told him that the doorman had recovered his wits enough to come after him, but Tyrone jerked up a hand and motioned the man to a halt. "Wait!" Tyrone snapped. "I want to talk to this man."

"But Mr. Tyrone... " the doorman said, clearly confused. "The way he came bustin' in here and all... I've already called the cops."

"Call them back," Tyrone said smoothly. "There's no need to involve the police in this, Jerry."

"Well... okay, Mr. Tyrone." The doorman sounded disappointed that he couldn't waltz a little with Hallam before the arrival of the authorities.

Hallam figured Myron Dart was in enough pain to not be a threat for a few minutes, anyway, so he got off of the man's wrist and said to Tyrone, "The way you're throwin' orders around, could be you own this place behind a front man or two."

Tyrone slipped a cigarette in his mouth and lit it with a gold lighter. "Could be," he admitted. "Or maybe not. That's neither here nor there. What's your connection with Kevin Jeffries?"

Dart curled up on the floor, holding his injured wrist and making little moaning sounds. Hallam stepped around him and came closer to the table where Tyrone stood and Gail Sumner sat. Right from the start, there had been several ways of playing this. He could have been subtle and trailed Tyrone for a while, but that might have taken too long. The fracas with Myron Dart, short-lived though it had been, had cut right to the heart of things, and that was the way Hallam liked it.

"I'm lookin' for Kevin," he told Tyrone. "His boss hired me to find him. Seems the boy up an' disappeared."

"You're a private investigator?" Tyrone sounded surprised.

Hallam nodded.

"Lucas Hallam," Tyrone mused. "I believe I have heard of you after all, Mr. Hallam, now that I think about it." He reached inside his coat, and when Hallam tensed, Tyrone smiled and said, "Relax, Mr. Hallam. I'm reaching for my checkbook."

That wasn't what Hallam had expected. He wasn't prepared for what Tyrone said next, either.

"I'd like to hire you myself. I'll double whatever Dr. Bauer is paying you to find Kevin, on the condition that you notify me first."

Hallam blinked. "You want to hire me? Shoot, I figured you kidnapped the boy."

"Why in the world would I do that?" Tyrone sounded genuinely startled by the suggestion.

Hallam hesitated before answering. This hadn't gone like he had anticipated. He had figured Tyrone would get all huffy and deny knowing anything about Kevin Jeffries. Now, Tyrone not only wasn't running scared, he seemed to want Kevin found as much as Dr. Bauer and Elena Fleming did. There were only two possibilities, Hallam finally decided: either Tyrone was behind the boy's disappearance, in which case he already knew that Thornton Jeffries was Kevin's father, or Tyrone hadn't had anything to do with it. Either way, Hallam didn't see any harm in revealing the connection between Kevin and his father.

"The boy's daddy is Thornton Jeffries," Hallam said.

"Really?" Once again, Tyrone sounded honestly surprised. "I had no idea."

"Then why do you want him found?"

"The young man and I have, ah, some business dealings to conclude," Tyrone said.

"What kind of business does an astronomer have with a high-class owlhoot like you?"

Tyrone chuckled. "You misjudge me, Mr. Hallam, just like the members of the press and our local police departments do. I'm just a businessman, an entrepreneur, if you will. A promoter." He put a hand on the soft flesh of Gail Sumner's shoulder, which was left bare by the low-cut silvery gown she wore. The dress went well with her platinum hair and deep blue eyes. "At the moment, I'm promoting Gail here. You could say she's my current project. But only in a business sense, of course."

"Of course," Hallam agreed heavily, not believing that for a second. "That still don't tell me why you're lookin' for Kevin Jeffries, or how come that goon o' yours was lurkin' around his house."

"I'm afraid some things will have to remain confidential until the time is right to announce them, Mr. Hallam. That's the way of business, after all. Everything at the proper time." Tyrone gestured softly with the checkbook he had taken from his coat. "Now, about that offer I made to you... ?"

Hallam shook his head. "Don't think so. I already got a client. But I'll be keepin' an eye on you, Tyrone, so don't try nothin' funny." He jerked a thumb toward Dart, who had pulled himself into a sitting position but still had his sore wrist cradled in his lap. He was staring up at Hallam with hatred in his eyes. "And keep that fella clear of me, or next time there'll be worse trouble."

"Myron won't bother you anymore, Hallam. I can assure you of that."

Hallam turned to walk out. The club had cleared of patrons when the trouble started, leaving only the puzzled musicians on the bandstand to witness the confrontation between Hallam and Tyrone. He ignored the doorman's glare as he went out to his flivver, got in, and drove away.

Well, it had felt damned good to pop that Dart fella in the snoot, Hallam mused, but other than that, he couldn't see that he'd done a bit of good. Kevin Jeffries was still missing, and while the most likely suspect in his disappearance was not yet in the clear—Hallam wasn't stupid enough to take everything Tyrone had told him at face value—the waters had still been muddied up considerable. If Tyrone wasn't behind Kevin's kidnapping... hell, if there hadn't been any kidnapping at all... then where in blazes *was* the young astronomer? And if Tyrone had been telling the truth, what sort of connection could Kevin have with a shady character like Tyrone and a lovely young actress like Gail Sumner?

Elena Fleming was an actress, too, and pretty enough without being as spectacularly beautiful as Gail. Elena had never had the benefit of a publicity push like the one Gail was beginning to get, either. Other than that, there were some similarities. Maybe Kevin had a fondness for pretty young actresses, and maybe just because he was engaged to Elena, that didn't mean he might not be mixed up with somebody else like Gail. In which case Tyrone could have gotten wind of the affair and had the boy taken out and done away with. Men like Tyrone tended to get mighty possessive at times, Hallam knew, especially where women like Gail Sumner were concerned.

That would explain why Tyrone hadn't known about Kevin's father being Thornton Jeffries. If Tyrone had regarded Kevin solely as a romantic rival to be rubbed out, he wouldn't give a hoot who the youngster's father was. He'd just have Kevin killed and be done with it.

Hallam shook his head. He was doing a lot of speculating, but he couldn't prove a bit of it. Not only that, but the vague theory he'd come up with didn't really explain why Myron Dart, Tyrone's hired muscle, was hanging around Kevin's house. Dart's presence there made it look like Tyrone really was looking for Kevin. It was enough to make a fella's brain hurt, Hallam decided, and when that happened, the best thing to do was to head for the high country and clear your head.

He turned the flivver toward Pasadena. Mount Wilson was the closest thing he was going to find to the high country in these parts.

Evidently Dr. Bauer and his staff had finished their work for the night and gone home, because the parking lot around the observatory was empty when Hallam pulled in there an hour or so later. During the drive up here, he had been over and over the facts of the case, skimpy as they were, but he still couldn't make them add up to anything else other than the two possibilities that had already occurred to him—either Kevin Jeffries had been kidnapped by someone after a hefty ransom from his father... or Walter Tyrone had had the youngster killed in a fit of jealousy over Gail Sumner. That last theory was really stretching things, Hallam thought, but he couldn't afford to ignore it.

He parked his flivver, killed the engine, and got out. The observatory would give him a quiet spot to think, and it was certainly pretty up here. He had told Dr. Bauer that he didn't know much about the stars except how to steer by them, but that wasn't strictly true. Many a night on the trail, he had lain in his bedroll and watched the great canopy of the sky spread out above him. To anyone who had spent a great deal of their days and nights outdoors, the sky was a source of endless fascination. Hallam had always enjoyed looking up at the stars, and that was what he did now. Everyone from the ancients on down had known that there were pictures in the stars if you looked close enough. Hallam had seen them himself.

They were always shifting, ever changing, but they were there.

And if you got tired of one picture, you could always look at the stars from a little different angle and see a picture that was totally different....

That thought burst through Hallam's brain at the same instant as the great dome of the observatory began to slide open.

Hallam wheeled around in surprise, hearing the faint grinding hum of the electric motors that operated the dome. In the starlight filtering down, he saw the split opening up in the center to give the telescope within access to the night sky. He had thought the observatory was deserted, but that dome wouldn't be opening by itself.

Bauer had said that Kevin Jeffries was working on a project of his own, a special project that was potentially quite important.

Maybe Kevin had come back to the observatory to finish it up, Hallam thought as he started toward the domed building.

The door was unlocked, he discovered when he got there. That made sense; as an important assistant to the director, Kevin likely would have had a key to get into the place. Hallam slipped in as quietly as possible, and that was pretty quiet considering that he'd been taught how to move by an old Apache. However, the noise of the motors was louder inside, and it would cover up any faint sounds he made.

There was a small light burning off to one side of the telescope, but other than that the cavernous space was dark. A slender figure in a long white coat moved around over there, near the eyepiece, then bent to peer through it as the dome's aperture reached its maximum. The man straightened, made notes on a clipboard, looked through the telescope again.

Hallam ambled up behind him and said, "Howdy, Kevin."

The figure in the white coat yelped in shock, threw the clipboard up in the air, and spun around, backing up quickly against the unyielding mass of the telescope. Hallam recognized him from the description—the dark hair parted in the middle, the wispy mustache. He was Kevin Jeffries, all right, no doubt about that.

"Who... who are you?" Kevin asked with a gulp of nervousness.

"Name's Lucas Hallam. I been lookin' for you for a few hours now, but I got to admit it seems longer. You got a lot of folks worried about you, son. I figured you was either dead or kidnapped."

Kevin swallowed again. "You... you're looking for me? Why?"

"That's my job. I'm a private detective."

"Oh, God." Kevin's fright grew visibly. "You're not working for... for *her*, are you?"

"Her?" Hallam repeated, a frown of confusion on his face. "You mean Gail Sumner?"

"No! I'm talking about Elena!"

"Elena Fleming? Well, she's mighty worried about you, but she ain't footin' the bill for my services, if that's what's got you spooked. I'm workin' for—"

Hallam broke off as a sweeping beam of light washed through the door he had left open behind him and played over Kevin's face. Hallam jerked his head around in time to see the last flicker of the headlights as the car outside came to a stop.

Kevin yelped again, and as Hallam turned back toward him, the young man lunged toward the small lamp that was set up on a nearby table and swept it off onto the floor. The bulb broke with a popping sound and darkness fell over the interior of the observatory. Hallam heard the swift patter of feet as Kevin ran off into the gloom.

A flashlight beam lanced through the blackness. "Kevin?" a voice called. Hallam recognized it as belonging to Walter Tyrone. "Kevin, are you in here? Come on, lad, no one's going to hurt you."

Hallam bit back a curse and edged to the side. Maybe Tyrone had followed him up here, maybe the so-called promoter had come on his own. Either way, it didn't matter. What was important was keeping Kevin alive.

"Hallam?" That voice came from another part of the observatory, and Hallam knew its owner, too—Myron Dart. "You in here, Hallam? I saw your car outside, and you ain't gettin' out until you and I settle up for that poke in the snoot, you son of a bitch!"

"Take it easy, Myron," Tyrone snapped. "The important thing is finding Jeffries."

Hallam wished he'd brought the Colt from the car, but it was still in the glove box. He'd have bet the farm that both Tyrone and Dart were armed.

"Walter, where are you? I don't like the dark!"

That complaint made Hallam's frown deepen. Gail Sumner? Had to be. But if Tyrone had come up here to kill Kevin Jeffries, he wouldn't have brought Gail with him, would he? Not unless he wanted to make sure she understood what would happen if she ever went behind his back with another man again. But Hallam had just about discarded that theory...

"Just stand still, Gail," Tyrone said impatiently as he swept the flashlight beam around. "If you want to do something to help, see if you can convince Kevin to come out."

"All right, I will," Gail Sumner said, and Hallam could hear the pout in her voice. "Kevin! Please, sweetie, nobody wants to hurt you. We just want your help, like you promised."

Tyrone added, "And if it's a matter of money, I don't mind increasing the payment, Kevin. How about a thousand dollars instead of five hundred?"

In the darkness, Hallam gave a little shake of his head. This was getting more confusing than ever. What could a young astronomer do that would be worth a grand to a slick operator like Walter Tyrone?

And when the answer occurred to him in the next instant as he remembered his conversation with Dr. Bauer, he muttered a heartfelt, "Oh, hell!"

That was a mistake. With a rush of footsteps, Myron Dart charged him, shouting, "Gotcha, cowboy!"

"Myron!" Tyrone yelled, but it was too late now.

Enough starlight filtered down through the opening in the dome for Hallam to make out the shape of Dart lunging toward him. He ducked under the wild round-house punch that Dart swung at his head and stepped closer to slam a fist into the thug's midsection. It was like punching the wood-paneled wall of the Red Top.

Dart grunted and flung his arms around Hallam in a bear hug. Both men went down.

Hallam twisted as he fell and managed to land on top of Dart. He brought a knee up, but Dart took the blow on the thigh. Dart growled, and Hallam felt his ribs starting to give a little as Dart increased the pressure. Hallam ducked his head and slammed the top of it into Dart's face.

Dart's nose must have been swollen and sore from the punch Hallam had landed earlier in the evening, because he let out a howl and loosened his grip enough for Hallam to get an arm free. He whipped another punch at Dart's face, aiming by instinct, and connected with the man's prominent jaw. Hallam's other arm came loose then from Dart's grip, and as he heaved himself up so that he was sitting on Dart's chest, he clubbed both hands together and lifted them over his head, ready to smash them down in a blow that would end this fight.

Lights came on all over the observatory, blinding Hallam. He heard Kevin Jeffries cry raggedly, "Enough! That's enough, dammit! I wish I'd never even seen that blasted star!"

Myron Dart suddenly bucked underneath Hallam, throwing him off. Hallam rolled and came up onto his feet as his vision started to settle down a little. Dart scrambled upright and jerked a gun from inside his coat. As he leveled the pistol at Hallam, Tyrone shouted, "No, Myron! Blast it, don't shoot him!"

Dart's hands trembled a little as he trained the gun on Hallam. "Aw, come on, Mr. Tyrone," he pleaded. "I got to!"

"No! This isn't like the old days, Myron. We're legit now, remember?"

Hallam stood very still as Dart struggled with the conflict between his instinct and his boss's command. Finally, he lowered the gun and muttered. "Hell, hell,

hell! You don't know how close you came, cowboy. You just don't know."

"Reckon I do," Hallam said, trying not to breathe too big a sigh of relief.

Kevin Jeffries strode out into the center of the floor toward Tyrone and Gail Sumner, who stood nervously with the promoter's arm around her shoulders. She had added a silver fox stole to her outfit and looked just as lovely as the last time Hallam had seen her.

"Legitimate," Kevin said with scorn in his voice as he faced Tyrone. "Does that include sending your strong-arm man to beat me up so I'd be sure to do what you wanted?"

"I've explained that, Kevin," Tyrone said, forcing himself to sound patient. "That was all a mistake."

"Ha! Reverting back to your true nature, I'd call it."

Hallam wanted to tell the boy to walk lightly around Tyrone and Dart, but Kevin was too mad to listen to him.

"Do you know how much trouble you've caused me?" Kevin demanded. "Do you have any idea how I've spent the past two days? I've been hiding! I sat in the bushes at Griffith Park most of the day today, and I'm covered with insect bites!"

Hallam knew Griffith Park and the Bronson Canyon area from the hundreds of Western pictures he'd worked on there as a stunt player and riding extra. But he never would have thought of looking for Kevin Jeffries there. It was a good thing he'd wandered back up here to Mount Wilson tonight on a hunch... maybe. He and Kevin weren't out of the woods yet.

Kevin put his haggard face in his hands and said around them, "The worst part has been dodging that crazy woman. I never should have told her what I'd found... and then you and that girlfriend of yours show up and make everything worse!"

Hallam came over and put a hand on Kevin's shoulder. Everything he had heard so far had confirmed the theory that had sprung into his mind earlier, but he had to know for sure. "You discovered a new star, didn't you, son?" he asked. Kevin nodded jerkily, and Hallam went on, "And since you found it, you get to name it."

"It's a perfect gimmick," Tyrone put in. "He names the star after Gail—one new star named after another one, get it? Hell, with something like that going for us, I can get Gail plenty of ink in every paper in town. Hell, across the whole damn world!"

"But Elena thought the star ought to be named after her," Hallam said. "After all, she's the gal you're engaged to, Kevin, so I reckon I can see her point."

"I am *not* engaged to her! She's the one who wants to get married, not me. But when I told her about the star, nothing would satisfy her until I'd promised to name it after her." Kevin swallowed and turned a sick gaze on Hallam. "She carries a gun, you know."

"I know. She pointed it at me earlier tonight." Hallam turned to Tyrone. "Look, you can't force the boy to name that star after Miss Sumner here, and you can't bribe him, either. He found the thing, and he's got the right to call it whatever suits his fancy."

"Oh, I wouldn't have minded naming it after her," Kevin said. "And the money would have come in handy, since I'm trying to stay independent of my father. It's just that Elena—"

"Yes, Kevin?" The new voice came from the entrance of the observatory. It was shrill and high-pitched and Hallam knew it was going to be nothing but trouble. "What about Elena?"

Everyone turned around sharply to face Elena Fleming, who stood just inside the entrance with the same pistol in her hand that she had threatened Hallam with in the kitchen of Kevin's house. Kevin's eyes widened in terror, and he ducked around the telescope, shouting, "Somebody stop her! She already took a shot at me yesterday!"

Elena jerked the gun toward the spot where Kevin had disappeared and pulled the trigger. With a wicked crack, the pistol sent lead ricocheting off the telescope while Hallam, Tyrone, Dart, and Gail Sumner dove for cover.

"You traitor!" Elena screamed at Kevin. "I thought you loved me, and then you tell me you're going to name *my* star after that... that hussy just for money!"

As he crouched on the other side of the telescope, Kevin protested, "But I told you that thug threatened me, Elena! I thought I had to go along with them or they'd kill me!"

She advanced steadily toward the massive apparatus, the gun unwavering in her hands. "I come up here hoping and praying that I'd find you safe—and then here you are with that... that woman! I'll show you who you should have been scared of! How dare you trifle with my affections?"

This whole mess had gone from dangerous to crazy back to dangerous, Hallam thought as he knelt behind one of the desks scattered around the big room. A few feet away, Dart was hiding behind another desk, and he had his gun out again. On the other side of the room, Tyrone and Gail had taken shelter behind a large rolling blackboard with a star chart pulled down from a roller at the top of it. Future editions of that chart might include a new star, Hallam thought, but Kevin Jeffries wouldn't get to name it unless somebody did something about Elena—and soon. There was no place else for Kevin to hide, and she would have a clear shot at him again in a matter of moments.

"Don't worry, boss," Dart called across the room to Tyrone. "I'll take care of that nutty dame!" He sprang to his feet, leveling his pistol at Elena.

Hallam didn't stop to think. Elena Fleming was more than a little touched in the head, no doubt about that, but Hallam couldn't stand by and watch her being gunned down. He launched himself across the space between himself and Dart and slammed into the back of the man's legs. Dart's pistol blasted, but the shot whined off into the shadows in the upper reaches of the dome, his aim ruined by Hallam. A split second later, Elena spun toward him and fired.

Hallam heard Dart grunt from the impact of the slug as he tumbled backward. There was a bloody patch on the shoulder of Dart's coat, and his face was pale. Hallam had seen more than his share of bullet wounds over the past fifty years or so, though, and he figured Dart would be all right if he got some medical attention fairly soon.

Kevin screamed as Elena fired again. Hallam raised himself enough to see that Elena had him cornered, backed up under the cylindrical body of the giant telescope until he couldn't go any farther. The next shot wouldn't miss.

Hallam scooped up the gun Dart had dropped when Elena shot him. He stood up, the pistol seeming to rise of its own accord as he lifted his arm. Elena was standing at an angle to him, pointing the gun in her hand toward Kevin. It was going to be a difficult shot, but Hallam didn't think about that. When there was a gun in his hand, Lucas Hallam didn't have to think. He just let his instincts take over and fired.

As it turned out, he missed, but only by a little. Shooting a gun out of somebody else's hand was a hell of a tricky proposition, no matter how often Tom Mix or Buck Jones did it in the movies. But the bullet grazed Elena's forearm, tearing the sleeve of her blouse, leaving a bloody streak on her arm, and making her drop the gun. That was just as good and, once Hallam stopped to think about it, even more spectacular than shooting the gun itself. Either way it got the job done, and as Elena reached for the fallen gun with her other hand, he got to her and kicked it across the room. She turned on him, screaming and hooking her fingers into claws, and he figured it was time to break that rule of his about not hitting women.

He clipped her on the chin with a loosely balled fist and she sat down hard, stunned.

"God Almighty!" Tyrone exclaimed as he peered nervously around the blackboard. "Are you all right, Hallam?"

Hallam's nerves were still jumping around like a barefoot kid on hot bricks, but other than that he was fine. He nodded and said to Kevin, who was staring in horrified fascination at Elena, "I reckon you'd better call the cops now, and an ambulance for ol' Myron over there. Hope none o' them slugs flyin' around here hurt that telescope."

Kevin gulped as he looked down at Elena. "Will...

will they lock her up?" he asked.

"For a while, I reckon they will. But they'll likely let her out again one of these days, so if I was you, son, I'd start thinkin' about who I was goin' to name that star after."

"He's going to name it after Gail, of course," Tyrone said as he emerged from behind the blackboard, bringing the obviously shaken actress with him, while a pallid-faced Kevin went over to Bauer's office to use the telephone.

"No!" Gail said abruptly, jerking away from Tyrone. She pointed a shaking finger at Elena and went on, "That lunatic would have come after me next! I don't want a star named after me, Walter, I really don't! Can't we just forget the whole thing?"

"But, baby, think of the publicity! You can't just throw away an opportunity like this!"

Hallam tucked the guns in his belt, hauled Elena to her feet, and went outside with her to wait for the cops and the ambulance. All the fight had gone out of her, and he didn't think she'd give him any more trouble. He left Tyrone and Gail squabbling behind him and stepped out to take a deep breath of the clean night air and look up at the stars.

Yep, there were still pictures up there, and as far as Lucas Hallam was concerned, the little pinpricks of light didn't even need names. The stories they told were enough.

Kevin Jeffries surprised them all, Hallam found out later. An old cowboy and private eye might never *be* a star, as far as the movies were concerned.

But he had one of the real things with his name on it, anyway.

MEDICINE TONGUE

L. J. Washburn's detective Lucas Hallam is a private eye whose beat is the world of silent movies, in which he also works as a stunt man and extra. Here he is in a tale of danger on the set...

HALLAM WAS WORRIED about the gag right from the start. "There's just too much that can go wrong," he said to the director, Curtis Dearborn, when he cornered Dearborn in the studio commissary that morning before the trucks left for Bronson Canyon. "Nobody's ever jumped a stagecoach over a gully like that."

Dearborn sipped from the paper cup of coffee he held in one trembling hand while he raked the fingers of the other hand through his hair. The director looked like hell, Hallam thought, with dark circles under his eyes and a greenish tinge to his skin that testified to how bad his hangover was. The way Hallam heard it, Dearborn had been putting away plenty of bathtub gin at the Hollywood speaks he frequented these days. There was a lot of pressure on him to bring in a successful picture, since the studio was rumored to be suffering from financial troubles lately.

"Relax, Lucas," Dearborn said. "It's going to go off like clockwork. Now, if you'll excuse me, I've got to see that all the equipment's loaded properly before we start."

Hallam bit back the objection that came to his lips. Dearborn was in no mood to listen to anybody's complaints. The director hurried off as Hallam stood there shaking his head. Hallam was glad he wasn't going to be on that runaway stagecoach; he was working as a riding extra in the picture, but he wasn't involved in any of the major stunt work.

Hallam was already in costume, if you could call it that. The buckskin shirt, denim pants, high-topped black boots, and broad-brimmed brown hat he wore belonged to him, not to the studio's costume department, as did the shell belt and holster in which his long-barreled Colt .45 rode. He'd worn that outfit or ones similar to it in dozens of pictures since settling down here in Hollywood back in 1916, and before that when he was riding the range for real as a Texas Ranger, deputy U.S. marshal, and Pinkerton agent. It had been said of Lucas Hallam that he was "the genuine article," but he never thought of himself that way.

He was just an old cowboy in a new-fangled world.

The caravan pulled out from the studio and headed for Bronson Canyon less than a half-hour later. It was still early in the morning, the sun barely up, but these location shoots were long, drawn-out affairs, cast and crew working from sunup to sundown some days to take advantage of the Southern California light. It didn't take long to reach the rugged, isolated area of Griffith Park where Dearborn's new picture had been shooting locations for a week now.

Hallam rode in a car with several more of the riding extras and cowboy stuntmen, among them his young friend Pecos. As usual, Pecos pestered him along the way to tell some of the stories of when he had been a gunfighter, but Hallam was in no mood for it today.

"I swear, Lucas, you're as touchy as an old silvertip grizzly today," Pecos said as the trucks and cars made their way to the canyons. "What's got you in such a bad mood?"

"Reckon I'm just a mite worried about the gag Dearborn's got planned," Hallam replied.

"The stagecoach jump? It'll be fine. I wouldn't be doing it if I didn't think so."

Hallam's head snapped around. "I didn't know you were riding the coach."

"Well, I wasn't supposed to," Pecos admitted. "But Dick Singer asked me to fill in for one of the other fellas who took sick. I'll be doubling one of the passengers inside the coach."

"Son of a bitch," Hallam muttered under his breath.

"It'll be all right, Lucas," Pecos said with the confidence of youth. "Shoot, I've jumped horses off cliffs and out of burning buildings. I reckon I can handle riding in a stagecoach."

"You be careful anyway," Hallam warned him.

Pecos's grin was cocky. "You ever know a stuntman who wasn't?"

Hallam didn't answer that.

The stagecoach gag was the first scene on the shooting schedule, and the crew got busy setting it up as soon as the trucks arrived at the location. Hallam wasn't involved in the shot, so he walked up to the top of a hill overlooking the area and studied the layout.

The stage road ran down the hill to his left at a fairly steep angle, bottoming out at the base of the slope and then rising again for a few yards until it reached a dry wash about ten feet wide.

Until today, the gully had been spanned by a sturdy wooden bridge, and hundreds of stagecoaches had clattered over it during the years that Western pictures had been shot here at Bronson Canyon. Now, though, the bridge had been dismantled for the most part. The remains of it had been carefully strewn around to resemble wreckage.

Later, after all the location filming had been done, the gimmick and gadget boys back at the studio would build a miniature mockup of the bridge as it usually looked and blow it up with a small charge of powder while being filmed.

When all the film was edited together, it would look on the screen as if the bridge blew up after the stagecoach had started rushing down the hill toward it. Since the villains of the story would be chasing the coach on horseback, the hero, who was handling the reins, would have no choice but to continue on down the hill, building up speed until the team would be able to leap over the ruined bridge and haul the stagecoach with them to land safely on the other side of the wash.

The short incline leading up to the bridge would serve as a natural ramp. The horses were specially trained jumpers and ought to have no trouble making the leap, especially since the wagon tongue that would normally be connected to the stagecoach would be disconnected and shortened slightly. It wouldn't be too noticeable on film, but the horses wouldn't actually be pulling the coach, which was custom-built so that a gasoline engine could be installed in it.

A driver concealed inside the coach would actually control it, looking out through nearly invisible eye-slits cut into the front of the stagecoach body. Approaching the jump, the driver would give the "stagecoach" enough gas to carry it over the gully without running into the horses from behind.

It was the most ambitious, complicated gag Hallam had ever seen. Curtis Dearborn was a director who liked realism, which had caused a few problems in the past. There would be a stuntman atop the coach, pretending to be the jehu, and the passengers inside would be stunt players, too, instead of the dummies that were sometimes used. Hallam had to admit that if it came off as planned, it would look downright spectacular on screen.

He walked along the crest of the hill toward the road. The phony stagecoach was parked there, and the boss stuntman was checking everything out. Hallam came up to him and asked, "How's it look, Dick?"

Dick Singer nodded. He was a wiry, middle-aged cowboy wearing a colorful shirt that was padded in the shoulders to make him look as big as the star he would be doubling in this scene. Singer would handle the reins during the gag. Along with the man who would actually drive the mock stagecoach, Singer's job was the most important, because he had to keep the team moving straight and fast down the hill to keep them from being overrun by the motorized vehicle. He slapped the side of the coach and said, "Looks fine to me, Lucas. Sure you don't want to come along for the ride?"

Hallam shook his head in response to Singer's grinning question. "The studio don't have that much money."

Pecos stuck his head out the coach window. "It's going to be fun, Lucas," he urged. "Not to mention a part of history. Nobody's ever done a gag this elaborate before."

"Nor one as dangerous, either," Hallam pointed out.

"Now, Lucas, you told me about how you shot it out with Paco Gomez's gang in that saloon in Amarillo when you were a Ranger. This can't be any worse than that."

"You're disrememberin' the facts, as usual. I had the county sheriff and damn near a dozen deputies backin' me up, and Gomez's bunch were too drunk to stand up, let alone shoot straight. They gave up pretty peaceful-like—"

"You're right, that's not the way I remember it," Pecos broke in. "Not the way I want to remember it, anyway. Come on, Lucas."

Hallam shook his head stubbornly. "Nope. If you've got your mind set on doin' this, you go right ahead, but I don't want no part of it."

"Suit yourself, Lucas," Dick Singer said as he swung himself up onto the driver's box and took up the reins. "You'd better step back out of camera range."

Dearborn was using three cameras—one on the hillside above the gully, one on the floor of the wash itself, and one on the far side. Three cameras were an expensive luxury, especially considering the studio's shaky financial ground, but Dearborn had persuaded the executives to spring for the extra cameras for this shot. Odds were they would only get one chance at capturing it on film.

Dearborn was standing near the camera positioned in the wash. He lifted a megaphone to his mouth and called, "All right, places, everyone! You all know what to do, so let's get a great take out of this, shall we? Do we have speed?"

"Speed!" the cameraman shouted back.

"Action!" Dearborn cried.

The hidden driver inside the coach already had the engine cranked up. Dick Singer slapped the reins down on the backs of the six-horse team, and they lunged forward against their harness. At the same instant, the real driver fed some gas to the engine, and the coach lurched ahead. It was a little jerkier than normal, Hallam thought as he watched from several yards away, but not so much so that it would be noticed by the audiences in the theaters, eager to be entertained in exchange for their nickels and dimes.

The coach rattled down the slope toward the wrecked bridge. Singer whipped the team and shouted, then looked back over his shoulder. Half a dozen men on horseback boiled over the top of the ridge, pursuing the coach down the hill. They were the heavies, clad in black for the most part, shooting off the blanks in their six-guns and whooping at the tops of their lungs even though there was no sound in the picture.

Hallam had heard rumors that within a few years the studios were going to start using sound pickups when they were filming, and he had to admit that scenes like this would be even more effective if the audience could hear the heavy booming of the guns and the pounding of the hoofbeats. Hallam wasn't sure he'd live to see the day when the moving pictures talked too, but if he did, it would be something to see—and hear.

Despite his apprehension, he found himself getting caught up in the excitement. It was a thrilling scene, no doubt about that. Singer and the inside driver, a man named Powell, Hallam remembered, were working together with perfect coordination. It looked for all the world like the horses were really pulling the stagecoach. They were running faster than usual, since they didn't have to pull the weight of the coach, and the vehicle was racing down the slope behind them.

Hallam could almost hear the fans gasping and shouting in darkened theaters all over the country when this picture played. During the jump itself, the camera in the wash might capture the fact that the tongue wasn't really attached to the coach, but it would be over so quickly that the audiences wouldn't even notice it in their excitement.

That was the way it usually was, Hallam thought. Folks saw what they wanted to see.

The coach reached the bottom of the hill and started up the short incline to the bridge. Hallam heard the hidden engine roar even louder as Powell poured on the gas. Singer held the team on a line straight as an arrow, and then they were at the brink of the wash, leaping up and out with precision and power and grace....

Even with all the noise going on, Hallam heard the sudden terrified shout from Dick Singer and then saw the stagecoach plummet into the wash.

It crashed head-on into the far bank of the gully, the coach splintering on impact. The horses had made the jump safely, but the falling stagecoach dragged them back over the edge, and they fell the dozen feet to the bottom with shrill, frightened whinnies that turned into screams of pain as bones snapped and shattered.

Dust billowed up from the bottom of the dry wash, and Hallam couldn't see a thing anymore. He could hear the wild shouts coming from all over the location, though, as he began running down the hill as fast as his long legs would carry him.

His pulse pounded inside his skull. Pecos had been in that coach, and the whole damn thing had come apart when it hit the wash. The coach had been sturdily built, but it hadn't been constructed to survive an impact like that. No telling how many of the men inside had been killed.

One thing was certain. Hallam had seen Dick Singer caught between the coach and the bank of the gully, and there was no way the stuntman could have survived the crash.

Hallam joined the rush of people into the gully, sliding down the near bank. Curtis Dearborn and his cameraman and assistant director had been the closest and had already pulled several victims from the wreckage. The AD was helping one man to sit down not far away, while the cameraman crawled into what was left of the coach. Dearborn stood waving his hands and shouting hoarsely, "Stay back, everybody stay back! Give us some room!"

Hallam bulled past the director and reached out to lend a hand as the cameraman helped Pecos out of the coach. The youngster had a cut on his forehead that was bleeding freely and was holding his right arm tight against his body with his other hand, but other than that he seemed unharmed.

Hallam slipped an arm around his waist to support him. "Come on, boy, let's get you away from here," Hallam said.

"What happened, Lucas?" Pecos asked in a choked voice. "What went wrong?"

"I don't know. How bad are you hurt?"

Pecos touched his bleeding head as Hallam lowered him to the ground at the side of the wash. "I've got this scratch, and my other arm's bunged up some. Maybe broke."

"Broken bones heal, and so do scratches," Hallam assured him. "You sure you're not busted up inside?"

Pecos shook his head. "I don't feel a thing wrong."

"Well, you're damned lucky." He glanced at the wreckage, where folks were still buzzing around like bees after a piece of watermelon. "A whole heap luckier than Dick Singer."

"Dick!" exclaimed Pecos, trying to struggle to his feet only to be held down by a gentle but firm hand on his shoulder from Hallam. "What happened to Dick, Lucas?"

"I saw him fall in front of the coach just before it hit. I reckon he didn't make it, kid."

Pecos shook his head, tears running down his cheeks and cutting trails in the dust that coated his face. "I just don't understand it," he said in a wretched voice. "Everything was worked out ahead of time. Nothing should have gone wrong."

Hallam glanced at the wreckage again. Like he had told Pecos, he didn't know exactly what had happened here in Bronson Canyon.

But he intended to find out.

"Mr. Hallam! Could I talk to you, please?"

———

THE VOICE CAME from behind Hallam and Pecos as they walked across the studio parking lot toward Hallam's flivver. It was late afternoon, and they had spent the day in the studio's infirmary. The cut on Pecos's forehead was stitched up and covered with a bandage that caused his hat to sit awkwardly on his head, and his right arm was in a sling. It had been determined that the arm was not broken, though, so Pecos hadn't been sent on to one of Los Angeles's hospitals, the way some of the other victims had.

Miraculously, only Dick Singer had been killed in the crash, although everyone inside the coach was injured to some extent. One man had two broken legs, a broken arm, and a shattered collarbone, but he was the most badly hurt of the bunch. He'd been insisting as he was loaded into the ambulance that he would be healed up in time to work on the next picture on the schedule, too, which hadn't come as any surprise to Hallam.

Cowboy stuntmen were some of the toughest—and stubbornest—hombres on the face of the earth.

Right now, though, Pecos didn't look very tough, and Hallam wanted to get the boy home so that he could rest. He wasn't happy about the delay as he turned around to see who was calling to him.

An attractive blond woman in a dark blue dress and a hat the same shade hurried toward him and Pecos. She looked vaguely familiar to Hallam and he knew he had seen her around the lot, but he didn't know who she was. As she came up to them, she said, "You are Lucas Hallam, aren't you?"

"That's right," Hallam rumbled. "Is this important, ma'am? Because if it ain't—"

"Oh, it's very important," the woman said. "You work as a private detective in addition to your job as a stunt-man, don't you?"

"I've got a P.I. license, take a case every now and then," Hallam admitted, trying to curb his impatience. He glanced at Pecos beside him. The youngster was pale and tired-looking, but he was all right for the time being.

"Very good. I want to hire you."

"Hire me? To do what?"

"To investigate that horrible accident out at Bronson Canyon this morning. I understand you were there."

"Yep, and so was this young fella here. In fact, he needs to get home—"

"This won't take but a minute," the woman insisted. She was pretty in a wholesome, cheerful way, although she didn't look very happy at the moment. "I should introduce myself. I'm Phyllis Dearborn."

Hallam frowned in surprise. "Curtis Dearborn's wife?" he asked before he could stop himself.

"That's right, although that situation may change momentarily."

"Sorry," muttered Hallam. He had heard the backlot gossip about how Dearborn's wife was planning to divorce him. That was another reason Dearborn had been hitting the speakeasies lately, according to the grapevine, along with the pressure from the studio.

Divorce was hard on a movie career, although a director could recover from it easier than an actor could.

The public seemed to care less about the private lives of the folks behind the cameras.

"That's quite all right. I'm not speaking to you as Curtis's wife now, Mr. Hallam. I'm here representing the Hollywood Animal Protective League. I'm the president of the organization, you know."

Hallam just nodded, although he hadn't known any such thing. He moved in a lot different circles than society ladies like Phyllis Dearborn.

"I want to hire you on behalf of the League," she went on. "I'm sure you've heard of us and the work we do to help prevent the injury and maiming of poor defenseless animals during the filming of motion pictures?"

That rang a bell for Hallam. There were several such organizations here in Hollywood, all of them trying to improve the conditions for animals on movie sets. Their targets were usually Westerns and historical epics because of all the horses involved in most of those productions. By and large, the cost-conscious studios hated the animal protection groups, since the measures demanded by the organizations were usually more expensive than the normal way of doing things.

"Listen, Miz Dearborn, I'd like to talk some more to you, but I got to get Pecos home—"

"Surely you know that all six of the horses involved in that accident this morning were so badly injured that they had to be destroyed," Phyllis Dearborn said sternly.

"Yes, ma'am, and I'm sorry—"

"Being sorry doesn't help those poor animals, does it, Mr. Hallam?"

"She's right, Lucas," Pecos put in. "Nothing worse than seeing a good horse have to be put down."

Hallam took a deep breath. Like most of the cowboys working in Hollywood, he felt a genuine fondness for the movie horseflesh. Every time he had to do a horse fall, he was careful not to put the mount in any more danger than was necessary. But that was just part of the business as far as Hallam was concerned. He was risking his own neck every time he yanked the wire for a Running W, too.

"What is it exactly you want, Miz Dearborn?" he asked.

"I want you to prove that that calamity was the result of carelessness and irresponsibility on the part of my husband. The League is going to file a lawsuit against Curtis and the studio on behalf of the owners of those horses, in hopes that barbaric practices such as this will not continue."

Hallam's weathered face creased even more in a frown. "You do know that a gent got killed in that crash, don't you? Dick Singer was a good hombre, a friend of mine. And this League of yours is goin' to court over some horses?"

Phyllis Dearborn had the good grace to flush a little in the fading sunlight. "Of course, we're very sorry about Mr. Singer. But he wouldn't have been killed, either, if Curtis hadn't been so stubborn. It's really his fault, not the studio's. Why, if you ask me, Curtis ought to be charged with murder."

"Murder?" Hallam repeated in surprise. "I didn't like that stunt, either, but the crash was an accident—"

"No," Phyllis Dearborn's voice was firm. "It was no accident, Mr. Hallam. That stunt was impossible, and Curtis knew it. Just ask Warren Gervin. Curtis did, and Warren told him it couldn't be done. But Curtis went ahead anyway, and now a man and six horses are dead. That's where I'd start the investigation if I were you, Mr. Hallam. I'd go talk to Warren Gervin."

"Haven't said I'd take the job yet," Hallam muttered.

"You will, though, won't you? The League wants to hire an investigator with some experience in these matters, and I'm told that you know a great deal about horses and stunts and things like that."

Pecos had to put his two cents in again. "Lucas knows more about most things than anybody else I know, ma'am."

Phyllis Dearborn lifted her chin and asked, "Well, Mr. Hallam, will you take the job?"

Hallam hesitated. He had to admit that what she had just told him was interesting. He was acquainted with the man she had mentioned, Warren Gervin, although he didn't know Gervin very well. Until a couple of years earlier, Gervin had been one of the top stuntmen in the business. Then an accident—a fall of two stories that could have just as easily killed him—had crippled Gervin and ended his career.

Hallam had heard that Gervin still did a little consulting work for some of the studios, and from the sound of what Phyllis Dearborn said, her husband had sought Gervin's advice on the stagecoach gag.

And if Gervin had warned the director against trying it, and Dearborn had gone ahead anyway... Well, Hallam could see how Dick Singer's survivors, as well as the owners of the destroyed horses, might have a case against Dearborn and the studio. Murder was still a pretty strong way of putting it, but sheer, reckless, damn fool stubbornness—that was more like it.

"Will you at least talk to Warren and make sure of what he told my husband?" Phyllis Dearborn asked.

Hallam nodded. "I reckon I can do that much. But I got to take this boy home first."

"Thank you, Mr. Hallam." She caught his hand in both of hers and shook it enthusiastically. "I know you probably think this is terrible and that I'm working against my own husband... well, my soon-to-be-ex-husband, I suppose you should say... but we really have to do something to make sure that tragedies like this don't ever happen again. Surely it can't help the picture business for Hollywood to ruthlessly slaughter helpless animals just because no one will take the time and trouble to speak up for those who have no tongues. Well, the animals do have tongues, of course, but they can't speak. That's what I mean."

"Yes, ma'am," Hallam said when she paused to take a breath. "I understand."

"Thank you again. I'll have a check for you, what-ever you like, when you report back to me." She handed him a card embossed with her name and an address and telephone number. "That's our home. Curtis isn't staying there anymore, so you don't have to worry about him being there if you visit or call. Just let me know as soon as you've talked to Warren Gervin."

"Yes, ma'am."

Phyllis Dearborn gave him a smile, said, "Good evening, young man," to Pecos, then turned and walked across the lot to a big Packard with a liveried chauffeur waiting behind the wheel. The driver hopped out, opened the rear door for her, then got in and drove off into the gathering shadows of dusk. Hallam watched the car leave the lot and vanish into the array of lights that were coming on all across Hollywood.

"That's one lady who likes to talk," Pecos said.

"A regular medicine tongue," Hallam replied quietly.

"What's that?"

"Indian name for somebody who talks all the time. Wonder if one reason her husband moved out is because his ears got tired."

"Pretty nice-lookin', though. For an older lady, I mean," Pecos added.

Hallam snorted. "Yep, she must've been ever' bit of thirty-five." He put a hand on Pecos's shoulder and steered him toward the flivver. "Come on, boy. Let's get you home, and then I'll go have me a talk with Warren Gervin."

Hallam took Pecos to the boardinghouse where the youngster rented a room and turned him over to his landlady, who promised to see that Pecos got some rest. Hallam left the boardinghouse and headed north into the hills.

He knew that Warren Gervin had a cottage up there on one of the narrow side streets off Mulholland. A few years earlier, Hallam had been to a party Gervin had given for some of the stuntmen in town. That had been before the accident that crippled Gervin, but Hallam hadn't heard anything about the man moving since then. He was pretty sure he could still find the place.

Twenty minutes later, he sent the flivver angling off Mulholland and followed a lane that looked familiar in the glow of the headlights. Gervin's cottage perched right on the edge of a hill, overlooking the vast spread of bright lights that made up Hollywood. Hallam saw the view beginning to appear as the trees around the lane thinned.

A car was parked in front of the small frame bungalow. Hallam's headlights swept over it. He brought the flivver to a stop, killed the engine, and stepped out.

Somebody inside the cottage yelled in pain and fear.

Hallam stiffened at the sound. Something wrong was going on in there, no doubt about that. He reached through the open window of the car and picked up the coiled shell belt and holster he'd put on the seat beside him earlier. He never went anywhere without some real cartridges in his pocket, so he slipped the Colt out of the holster, tossed the belt back into the car, and began thumbing shells into the cylinder as he trotted toward the cottage.

He'd never been one to stand aside from trouble.

Talking to Warren Gervin was his business right now, and if that meant busting up a fight, fine.

Hallam took the three steps up to the small porch in a bound as something crashed inside.

There were no lights burning, but the front door was open and Hallam could see the lights of the city through another open door at the back of the house. A pair of struggling figures blotted out those lights so that Hallam could dimly see their silhouettes. An arm rose and fell, and there was a loud, ugly thump.

"Hold it!" Hallam called.

One of the figures spun toward him, and a flash lit the room for an instant. The noise of a gunshot slammed against Hallam's ears as he threw himself to one side. He didn't know where the bullet went, but he hadn't been hit.

The gunman was still firing, though, trying to track Hallam through the darkness. A slug smacked into the wall near Hallam's head. Hallam triggered a shot in return as he struggled to his feet, but he couldn't tell if he hit anything. He was half-blinded by the muzzle flashes and half-deafened by the explosive reports in the small room.

Lights loomed on Hallam's right, and he realized he was next to a window. Without hesitating, he threw himself at it. If he could get out of the cottage, he thought, he could move around and maybe get behind the gunman.

Hallam had busted through dozens of saloon windows on movie sets, but those had been made of spun sugar and balsa wood. The real thing was a lot different and hurt a hell of a lot more when he crashed through the glass frame with his shoulder. But he was through and falling the short distance to the ground, rolling with the fall....

Rolling right off into empty air.

Hallam let out a startled curse as he realized that Gervin's cottage had been built even closer to the edge of the hill than he had thought. Then a split-second later, he slammed into the slope below him and kept rolling, crashing through the brush that covered the hillside. Branches clawed and scratched at his face as he tried to grab something and bring himself to a stop. Somehow he managed to hang on to his gun as he tumbled down the hill.

About fifty yards down the slope, Hallam finally brought his plunge to a halt. He hurt all over, but he ignored the pain and pulled himself to his feet. There was bad trouble at the cottage, and he had to get back up there.

Before he had gone more than twenty feet, though, he heard the slamming of a car door and then the frantic growl of an engine. Tires squealed and gravel spurted as somebody left in a hurry. Hallam tried to speed up his pace, but the slope was steep and thick with underbrush that held him back at every step. It was long, frustrating minutes before he reached the top of the slope again.

By that time the sound of the car's engine had faded away. Hallam found the open back door of the cottage and ran inside. "Gervin!" he shouted. "Gervin, you here?"

There was no answer. Hallam ran straight through the cottage to the front door and peered out. Sure enough, the car that had been next to his flivver was gone, just as he expected. Whoever had taken the shots at him had fled.

But what the hell had happened to Gervin?

A bad feeling grew in Hallam's belly as he remembered the thump he had heard just before the shooting started. It had been the sound of something hard hitting a human skull. Hallam had heard it all too many times in the past.

He fumbled around on the wall until he found a light switch and flipped it on. Squinting against the sudden glare, Hallam looked around the room. This was a combination living room and den, with a door leading into a small kitchen and then on out the back. The bedroom and bathroom were to the side, and that was all there was to the house. It took only a moment to search every room and confirm something that took Hallam by surprise.

He was alone.

He had expected to see Warren Gervin's crumpled, lifeless body when he turned the lights on, but no one else was in the cottage. There was a large smear of blood on the floor next to the kitchen door, though, and that was where he had seen the two figures struggling.

But the corpse, if there had been one, was gone.

———

HALLAM DROVE THROUGH THE NIGHT, still trying to ignore the aches and pains from the fall down the hill. The wheels of his brain were turning over rapidly. He knew he ought to stop at the nearest telephone and call Lieutenant Ben Dunnemore, his friend on the Hollywood homicide squad, because what had gone on tonight at Warren Gervin's cottage was sure as shooting either murder or attempted murder.

But that missing body had him worried.

He followed Mulholland back down into town and dug out the card Phyllis Dearborn had given him. By the light of a passing streetlight, he read the address on it and turned the flivver toward the neighborhood where the Dearborn house was located. He wanted to talk to her before he did anything else. There was a question he had to ask her.

Fifteen minutes later, Hallam pulled up in front of a large white house that sat at the top of a sloping, well-manicured lawn. He left the flivver at the curb and went up a curving flagstone walk to the front door.

Chimes sounded somewhere inside when he thumbed the bell.

A maid answered the door and gave him a dubious frown as he asked, "Is Miz Dearborn here? I need to talk to her."

"I'm not sure..." the maid began, and Hallam knew why she was hesitating. After that roll down the hill, his clothes were dirty and torn, and there were scratches on his face. He probably looked like some sort of lunatic. But it was important that he talk to Phyllis Dearborn.

"Just tell her that it's Lucas Hallam, and it's about her husband and Warren Gervin."

"Very well," the maid sniffed, leaving Hallam on the doorstep as she went to speak to her mistress.

The servant's attitude had changed a little when she came back a couple of minutes later. "Mrs. Dearborn wants to see you right away," she said.

She led him down a hallway into a parlor and left him there, and a moment later Phyllis Dearborn came in. She was wearing a long silk dressing gown that swirled around her ankles. She would have been breathtakingly lovely if she hadn't looked so worried.

"What is it, Mr. Hallam?" she asked. "I didn't really expect to hear from you again until tomorrow."

"Well, I started my diggin' tonight, ma'am. Your husband doesn't happen to be here, does he?"

She frowned in confusion. "No, I told you he hasn't been staying here since we separated."

"I just thought he might have stopped by...."

She shook her head emphatically. "No. Curtis knows that I don't want to see him anymore. Our lawyers do our talking for us now."

"But you do know where he's living now, don't you?"

"Well, yes," admitted Phyllis Dearborn. "I have his address and his new telephone number. It's an apartment over on Vine."

Hallam spotted a telephone sitting on a fragile-looking antique side table. He picked up the receiver and asked, "What's the number?"

Phyllis Dearborn looked as if she was going to be stubborn and not give it to him without an argument, but then she lifted her silk-clad shoulders in a pretty little shrug and recited the number. Hallam gave it to the operator, then listened as the telephone on the other end rang futilely twenty times.

He hung up and said, "Give me the address, and tell me any places your husband's been spendin' time lately."

"What is this about, Mr. Hallam?" She wasn't nearly as talkative tonight. Hallam's attitude and appearance, as well as his questions, obviously had her worried.

"I'm just tryin' to find out what your husband was doin' tonight."

"He's in more trouble, isn't he?" Phyllis Dearborn chewed her lower lip and managed to look attractive doing even that. "Curtis has done something else."

Hallam shook his head. "I don't know."

That was true as far as it went, but he had some suspicions. According to Phyllis, Warren Gervin had told Curtis Dearborn that the stunt Dearborn planned was not only impossible but dangerous. If Gervin testified to that in court, it would be enough to nail Dearborn's coffin shut. The director would be lucky if criminal charges weren't brought against him, and at the very least, his career would be ruined forever. Between the impending divorce, the damages he would have to pay, and the fact that no studio would ever hire him again, Curtis Dearborn would be penniless, with absolutely no prospects.

That was enough to drive a man to murder.

But first Hallam had to establish whether or not Dearborn had an alibi for the past hour or so. If he did, that would mean the intruder at Gervin's cottage had been someone else. Hallam wanted as much information as he could get before he turned everything over to Ben Dunnemore. And he still hadn't figured out why Dearborn—or anybody else—would carry off Gervin's body when they fled.

Phyllis Dearborn gave Hallam the address of her husband's new apartment and also the names of several speakeasies Dearborn had been known to frequent. It was clear that she was a little reluctant to part with the information. She might have been divorcing Dearborn, but some of the protective instincts born of a long relationship were still there. As Hallam started to leave, he paused in the door of the parlor and looked back at her.

"Maybe it's none of my business," he said, "but how come you and your husband split up?"

"I couldn't take being in second place anymore."

Hallam frowned. "I never heard anything about Dearborn havin' another woman."

Phyllis shook her head. "Not another woman. His movies. You worked for him, Mr. Hallam, you know how single-minded he was. He felt there was nothing he couldn't capture on film if he put his mind to it, and he worked to make it true. Unfortunately, in the process, he didn't have enough time left over for anything else in his life."

Hallam nodded slowly. That fit with what he knew

of Curtis Dearborn, all right. And it made the man's motive for murder even stronger. Dearborn had sacrificed his personal life for the movies, and he wouldn't give them up because of what Warren Gervin might say in the courtroom.

"None of the accidents on Curtis's pictures would have happened if he wasn't so stubborn," Phyllis went on. "Like I said, he thought he could find a way to film anything."

A thought suddenly occurred to Hallam. "That picture Gervin was workin' on when he was hurt—your husband was the director, wasn't he?"

"Yes, that was Curtis's picture."

"So Gervin wouldn't have had any reason to lie for him in court. Likely he would've enjoyed seeing your husband take the blame for Dick Singer's death."

"I... I don't know. It's true that Mr. Gervin was injured while doing a stunt for Curtis, but I never got any sense that he blamed Curtis"

"Well, we'll see," Hallam said. What he didn't say was that the noose seemed to be getting tighter and tighter around Curtis Dearborn's neck. Dearborn would have known that there was no way he could talk Gervin into changing his story to protect him.

Hallam nodded to Phyllis Dearborn and left the house. The lady probably wouldn't get much sleep tonight, what with all the worrying she was doing, Hallam thought.

But then he didn't plan on sleeping much, either.

———

NO ONE ANSWERED Hallam's knock on Dearborn's door. The lock wasn't a very good one, and Hallam was inside the apartment in a matter of minutes, looking around to confirm what he had suspected. Dearborn was gone. His clothes and things were still there, so he must have left in a hurry.

Well, Hallam thought, he hadn't expected to find Dearborn sitting there with Gervin's body. He left the apartment and relocked the door, then started making the rounds of the speakeasies. Hallam knew just about every speak in Hollywood, and over the next couple of hours he visited not only the ones Phyllis Dearborn had told him about but several others besides. No one in any of them had seen Curtis Dearborn that evening.

Hallam sighed as he got back into his flivver. He wasn't sure what he had intended to do if he caught up with Dearborn and the director didn't have an alibi. Hallam sure as hell wasn't going to help him cover up a murder. But he would have liked to hear what had happened from Dearborn himself.

Now there was nothing to do but turn the whole thing over to the cops.

Hallam found a telephone in a drugstore, called Ben Dunnemore at home, and gave the homicide lieutenant the whole story, starting with the disastrous stunt that morning. Dunnemore chewed him out for not reporting the trouble at Gervin's hillside cottage right away, but once Dunnemore was through with his grousing, he said, "I'll get some boys out there right away. You come by headquarters first thing in the morning, Lucas, and give me a statement. Maybe we'll know more by then. Gervin's body could turn up before morning."

"If he's dead," Hallam said.

"From what you told me," grunted Dunnemore, "he couldn't be anything but. Remember, first thing in the morning."

"I'll be there," Hallam promised.

Then he went back to his own apartment, but just as he had expected, sleep was a long time coming despite his weariness. There was just too much to think about, and his brain wouldn't let go of any of it. Sometime far into the night, Hallam finally dozed off, feeling as if there was an answer waiting for him, squirming away just out of reach of his fingertips every time he reached for it.

———

THE STUDIO WAS BUZZING with gossip when Hallam got there the next morning after stopping by the police station to give his statement to Ben Dunnemore. The guard at the studio gate told Hallam the same thing that Dunnemore had earlier—Curtis Dearborn was still among the missing, and so was Warren Gervin. If Dearborn had hoped to quietly dispose of Gervin and have it thought that the man had mysteriously disappeared, the plan had been ruined by Hallam's untimely visit to the cottage.

The guard also had a message for Hallam. The studio's production chief wanted to see him right away.

Hallam went to the big office building that sat in front of the sprawling shooting stages and was quickly ushered into the sanctum of J. Frederick Darby. The executive was a small, balding, deceptively mild-looking man who wielded more power than anybody else around here. He waved Hallam into a chair in front of the massive hardwood desk and said, "Good morning, Lucas. Thanks for stopping by. It's always good to see you, but this time I wish the circumstances were pleasant."

Hallam dropped his hat on the floor next to the chair and said, "I reckon you want to hear about Curtis Dearborn."

"That's right. I've heard the gossip, of course; it's impossible to keep anything a secret for very long in this town. But I want the straight story from you, Lucas."

Hallam gave it to him.

Darby leaned back in his chair and shook his head when the big cowboy was finished. "It doesn't look very good for Curtis, does it?" he said with a sigh. "He's gone off the deep end. I've always been afraid it would happen, the way he throws himself so whole-heartedly into his pictures. With that trouble with his wife, and the problems the studio has been having, it was just too much for him."

"Is the studio really in that much trouble?"

Darby grimaced and nodded. "We were counting on Curtis's new production to put us back in the black, and he knew it. I'm sorry now that I ever told him. That extra pressure may have been just what it took to make him snap. Now Dick Singer's relatives are going to sue, and there's a good chance we'll be ruined. I wish I could say otherwise, but..." Darby shrugged. "My chief accountant could tell you just how bleak the financial numbers are if he were here. That's another cross I've got to bear this morning."

Hallam shook his head. "Don't reckon I understand."

"Roy Henson—you know him, he's the head of the

accounting department—he called in sick this morning. Has pneumonia or some such. I talked to him myself, and my God, he sounded awful, not like himself at all. I don't know when he'll be back. So everything seems to be falling apart at once." Darby sat up and brought a clenched fist down on the desk, an uncharacteristically emphatic gesture for him. "I'll tell you what's causing it, Lucas. It's this obsession with sound. If people would just leave the picture business alone and let them remain silent, the way God intended, then we wouldn't be having so much trouble."

Hallam didn't say anything, but he doubted if God cared much whether or not the movies talked. Seemed to him like a pretty frivolous subject to occupy the Almighty's attention.

"If there's anything I can do to lend a hand, you just let me know," he said to the production chief as he stood up to leave the office.

Darby stood up as well and shook hands with him across the desk. "Thank you, Lucas. We'll be picking a new director today to try to salvage what we already had in the can on Curtis's picture, so you'll be notified when we're ready to start shooting again."

Hallam nodded his thanks and went back outside. It was a pretty day, but he doubted if Curtis Dearborn was paying much attention to the weather, wherever he was holed up.

A figure limping along toward one of the huge stages caught Hallam's attention. "Hey, Stan, hold up a minute," Hallam called as he trotted across the lot.

Stan Powell, who had been driving the motorized stagecoach the day before, turned to wait for Hallam. When he came up to the stuntman, Hallam went on,

"Didn't expect to see you around here today. Figured you'd still be in the hospital."

"They released me a little while ago, and I came straight over here," Powell replied. He was a medium-sized man in his forties with bruises on his face and a heavy bandage around his right ankle. "I wanted to see if I could figure out what happened."

"How're you feelin'?" Hallam asked, not surprised that Powell wanted to find out what had caused the accident. He wouldn't have expected any less from a stuntman. Hallam didn't know the man very well, since Powell usually did car gags and seldom worked on Westerns, but like most stuntmen, he was stubborn.

"I'm all right, I suppose," Powell said with a nod and a smile. "Banged my head a little, but you know it takes a lot to dent a stuntman's skull. And I sprained my ankle during the crash, but it's okay."

"You were lucky."

"We all were," Powell said, his tone more solemn now. "All of us except Dick."

Hallam fell in step beside Powell as they walked toward the back of the lot. "Got any idea what happened?" Hallam asked.

Powell shook his head. "Not really."

"Reckon the coach just didn't have enough steam to make that jump."

"No, that's not it," Powell said without hesitation.

Hallam looked over at him, eyes narrowing. "You're sayin' the gag could've worked?"

"Hell, yes, it could've worked. Nearly did. But the motor started cutting out when we went up the incline toward the bridge. It gave out entirely just before we got there. That's why our speed dropped and we didn't make it across."

Hallam hadn't noticed the speed of the mock stage-coach dropping dramatically, but he had been at the top of the hill, not inside the vehicle trying to coax it through the dangerous jump. And it probably wouldn't have taken much of a drop to cause the coach to crash, he thought.

"So it was a mechanical failure, rather than the stunt itself, that caused the wreck?"

Powell shrugged as he limped along. "Well, I can't say that for sure. Maybe we wouldn't have made it even if the engine hadn't cut out. But the way it was, there was no way in hell we were going to clear that wash."

"How come you didn't try to stop when the engine cut out?"

"I did. That's how my ankle got sprained. I had my foot jammed against the brake pedal. Didn't do any good."

"So you were going too fast to stop but not fast enough to make it across the gully?"

"That's right," Powell said. "Why all the questions, Lucas?"

Hallam looked at him again. "You haven't heard about Dearborn and Warren Gervin?"

"I told you, I came straight here from the hospital. What's this about Dearborn and Gervin?"

Hallam gave him a quick version of the story, and Powell let out a low whistle of surprise. "Sounds like Dearborn's gone loony, all right," Powell said.

"What about Gervin? He told Dearborn the stunt couldn't be done."

Powell shook his head and said, "I'm not surprised.

Nothing against Warren, you understand, but after that accident a couple of years ago, he... lost his nerve, I guess you could say. He was too crippled up to do any gags, of course, but some of the studios would come to him and ask him for advice on stunts they had planned. Warren always told them the gags were too dangerous, no matter what they were. Even if he hadn't been injured too badly to get back into stunt work, he would have turned down anything that was offered to him. Just too scared, you know what I mean?"

Hallam nodded. He'd known other men like that, men who had made their living with a gun until their fears caught up to them. They were never any good after that.

"There it is, what's left of it," Powell said, pointing. They had reached the rear of the lot, and the remains of the wrecked stagecoach sat there on a trailer behind some unused scenery flats. It barely looked like a stage-coach anymore.

Hallam watched while Powell began poking through the wreckage. The motor was located under the driver's box. The hatch that allowed access to it was crumpled, but with Hallam's help Powell managed to pry it open. He started going over the tangled mess of machinery inside.

"Lucky the whole thing didn't catch on fire and blow up," Powell commented after a few minutes. "Gas line's broken, and the fuel tank's probably ruptured, too."

Hallam leaned over and looked underneath the coach, seeing the gaping hole in the gas tank that had been concealed under the floor. If it had exploded, everyone inside would have been burned to a crisp, including Pecos. Hallam felt a surge of anger. Even if the stunt had been possible, as Powell claimed, Dearborn never should've taken the risk. Hallam reached up through the hole in the tank and brought his fingers out, smelling the gas and making a face. Maybe he was old-fashioned, but there was a lot to be said for horses. They never blew up, for one thing.

Rubbing some grit from the gas tank off his fingers, Hallam searched for the brake lines. They were snapped, of course. They had probably broken when Powell jammed on the brakes. Not that surprising, considering the speed the coach had been making when it reached the bottom of the hill in Bronson Canyon. Just another indication that not enough planning and preparation had gone into the stunt.

"Well, there aren't any answers here," Powell said discouragingly. "I guess we'll just have to chalk it off as general mechanical failure."

"Reckon so," Hallam agreed.

And yet... the thought that had been jumping around in his brain the night before was there again, tantalizing him with its nearness, then fading away again. He shook his head. This was nothing but a tragic accident, he told himself. He had been there and seen it for himself. An accident, followed by more tragic twists of fate.

But sometimes, Hallam suddenly realized, what the eye saw wasn't what really happened.

And nobody knew that better than somebody who created illusions

for a living.

———

NIGHT HAD SETTLED down over Hollywood again, and Hallam was waiting. The cops had put seals on the front and back doors of Warren Gervin's cottage, but not the windows. With Gervin presumed dead and a bulletin out for Dearborn's arrest, nobody expected anyone to show up here.

Nobody but Hallam.

He heard the sound of the car's motor several minutes before it crept up to the cottage, moving slowly without lights along the narrow lane. Hallam stood in the living room, gun in hand, while the car stopped and the driver got out. The shadowy figure came around the side of the bungalow and climbed awkwardly through the same window Hallam had used.

Hallam moved to the light switch, flipped it up.

He had his eyes slitted against the sudden glare, but the other man didn't. The man let out a startled cry and reached frantically under his coat. Hallam eased back the hammer of his Colt and said harshly, "Don't do it, Gervin!"

The overhead light revealed a short man grown thick around the middle. His bushy hair had gone gray since Hallam had seen him last, but the man was definitely Warren Gervin. He blinked, eyes still watering from the unexpected light, and took his hand slowly away from the butt of the pistol Hallam saw tucked into his belt.

With hate burning in his eyes, Gervin said, "I should have stuck around last night and made sure you were dead."

"That's right," Hallam agreed. "But you didn't, and now you're goin' to have to stand trial for murderin' Dick Singer and Roy Henson."

Gervin shook his head. "I don't know what you're talking about. Everybody knows you're a crazy old coot, Hallam."

"We'll see about that. The cops already know about the sugar you put in the gas tank of that gimmicked-up stagecoach so the motor would cut after it had run a little. You knew it'd be taken out to the location on a trailer and not started up until Dearborn was ready to shoot the gag. You left some marks when you tampered with those brake cables, too. You never figured anybody would look close enough to find the sugar or the sabotage. It would all be written off as an unfortunate accident."

"You can't blame that crash on me," Gervin insisted. "I told Dearborn not to try that stunt!"

"Yep, you did. But you knew it could be done. You just wanted to be able to testify in court that you warned him against it. You knew somebody would sue him and the studio over the crash. If the studio went belly-up because of the lawsuit, so much to the good, but what you really wanted was to see Dearborn ruined. You blamed him for the accident that cost you your career—and your nerve."

"There's nothing wrong with my nerve!" snapped Gervin.

"Reckon you didn't lose all of it, or you wouldn't have been able to sneak into the studio and dope the gas tank and fray the brake lines on that coach. You knew it'd crash, but you didn't plan on Dick Singer dyin', did you? You should've known you'd be taking a chance with the lives of all the stuntmen on it."

"You can't prove any of this," Gervin said scornfully.

"No, but Roy Henson could, since he was working

with you, feeding you inside information about the money troubles the studio was havin'. I don't know how you forced him to do it, but you had some sort of hold over him. Maybe he was skimmin' some cream off the top himself, and you knew about it. That'd explain some of the problems the studio was havin'. Henson panicked, though, when the crash was a lot worse than what you told him it'd be. He came up here last night and told you he was goin' to the cops. You had to shut him up." Hallam paused. "And that's when I came along."

"You son of a bitch," Gervin said fervently. "Nobody would have missed Henson. He didn't have any friends, any family, just his account books. He could've dropped out of sight and nobody would've given a damn."

"Reckon that must've been you who called Fred Darby this mornin' and pretended to be Henson."

"I couldn't just leave him here," Gervin said. "I couldn't have his body found in my cottage." He was breathing heavily now, and the look of a trapped animal was in his eyes.

"So you hauled him off while I was fallin' down the hill," Hallam said. "You stashed the body somewhere and holed up, waitin' to see what was goin' to happen. Worked out just fine for you, didn't it? The cops figured you were dead and that Dearborn killed you. I thought the same thing myself for a while, till I realized there was no proof you were even dead. And that got me to thinkin' about who it could be who really died here last night. I had a talk with Darby this mornin' and took a look at that wrecked stagecoach with Stan Powell, and things started fittin' together."

Gervin shook his head. "You can't prove it. You can't

prove anything. I can turn and walk out of here right now, a free man."

Ben Dunnemore said from the kitchen doorway behind him, "I don't think so, Mr. Gervin."

The former stuntman spun around, and despite Hallam's earlier warning, his hand darted toward the gun in his belt. He let out a crazed cry, and Hallam knew he was going to try to shoot his way out. Hallam sprang forward, lashing out with the Colt in his hand. The barrel thudded against Gervin's head.

Gervin folded at the knees, his pistol falling unfired from his fingers.

Dunnemore motioned to the officers who came out of the kitchen with him, and Gervin was picked up and taken out of the cottage, his hands cuffed behind him even though he was still stunned. The lieutenant turned to Hallam and said, "You were right, Lucas. And the case is going to be a lot easier to prove since you got Gervin to admit what he did. He'll break down and tell us where to find Henson's body, I'm sure of it. But I still don't know why I let you talk me into this setup. Somebody could've gotten hurt."

"Stuntmen are all crazy, Ben," Hallam said with a grin. "You know that."

Curtis Dearborn turned up three days later after a bender in Tijuana and was shocked to learn that the cops had considered him a murder suspect for a while.

Warren Gervin's conviction for Henson's murder and the manslaughter of Dick Singer muddied up the court proceedings until all the lawsuits against Dearborn and the studio were thrown out. Dearborn was unable to get more work anyway, and his wife divorced him. Hallam lost track of him after a while and couldn't bring himself to be too sorry. Dearborn had brought a lot of his troubles on himself, and the way Hallam saw it, Phyllis Dearborn deserved better.

He saw her every now and then, leading some protest about how animals were treated in the movies, and from what he heard, she was as much of a medicine tongue as always. She was like talking pictures, Hallam thought, an idea that was coming whether anybody wanted it or not. But whatever happened, the movies would survive. Hallam was sure of it.

LADYSMITH

"Ladysmith", an adventure from Hallam's days as a Pinkerton agent that finds him delivering a legacy for an old friend who has passed away, a chore that has him riding right into unexpected danger.

THE BAD NEWS—AND the package—caught up to Hallam in El Paso.

He had a room in the Camino Real Hotel downtown, a pretty fancy place for a man like him to be staying, but the client was paying for it. The fella owned a silver mine across the border in Mexico, and he had paid the Pinkerton Agency to find out who was responsible for high-grading some of his ore. Hallam was the agent given the job. He'd spent a week ferreting out the thieves, then returned to El Paso and wired the head office in Chicago to inform the boss of his success. He was waiting for a return telegram letting him know what his next assignment was going to be, so in the meantime he staked out his claim on a table in the bar. He was sitting there nursing a beer, long legs stretched out in front of him, when one of the desk clerks from the hotel lobby came over to him.

"*Señor* Lucas Hallam?" the man asked. He carried a long white envelope and a package wrapped in brown paper.

"That's me," Hallam said.

"These were delivered for you." The clerk placed the envelope and the parcel on the table.

Hallam handed the man a coin and said, "Much obliged." He waited until the clerk was gone before picking up the envelope. His name was typed neatly in the middle of it. Up in the corner, the name of a Santa Fe law firm was printed. Hallam had never heard of them before.

He frowned. Why would a lawyer be looking for him? Only one way to find out, he decided. He tore open the envelope and unfolded the sheet of paper inside. Enough afternoon sunlight came through the glass doors on the other side of the bar for him to read what was written on the paper.

It was a letter from one of the members of the law firm, informing him that one of their clients, a Mrs. Rose Taggart, had passed away. Hallam wasn't sure who that was until he noticed that the late Mrs. Taggart had resided in the town of Raton.

"Red Rosie?" Hallam muttered to himself. He thumbed back his hat. "Red Rosie's dead?"

It didn't seem possible. The last time he'd seen her, she had seemed perfectly healthy. She was in her thirties, about the same age as Hallam. Of course, she was in a line of work that didn't promote long lives, but she had managed to buy her own house so she wasn't just a soiled dove anymore. She was a madam.

That was like saying that just because he was a Pinkerton agent now, instead of a hired gun, his own life was safe as houses, Hallam thought.

There was more to the letter. The law firm was handling Rose Taggart's estate, and one of the bequests in her last will and testament had gone to her old friend Lucas Hallam. The item in question was enclosed in the package accompanying the letter.

Hallam set the letter aside. So whatever was in that package was his legacy from Red Rosie. He was surprised that she would have left him anything. They had enjoyed a few romps together, and he supposed she had considered him a friend. He slipped out his knife, cut the string around the package, and began to unwrap it.

Inside a couple of layers of paper, he found a hinged box of polished hardwood about eight inches long, six inches wide, and three inches deep. A simple catch kept the box closed. Hallam unfastened it and raised the lid.

Inside, nestled on a bed of red velvet, was the gun.

He recognized it as a Smith & Wesson .22 caliber revolver. A small brass plate on the inside of the box lid had the word *Ladysmith* engraved on it. The body of the gun had a nickel-plated finish on it, and the curved butt was made of ivory. Hallam took the gun out of the box, his big hand nearly swallowing it up.

He was accustomed to the heavy Colt .45 that he always carried. This little gun was nothing but a toy, a trinket. And yet there was a sleek, almost beautiful wickedness about it, a sense that if handled correctly, it could be dangerous indeed.

Sort of like its late owner, Hallam thought with a faint smile. Rose Taggart had been the same way.

Ladysmith was a good name for a gun like this. If ever there was a lady's gun, this was it. Hallam hefted the revolver. It felt very light as it lay on his palm.

Why in blue blazes had Rose left this gun to him? He had no use for it, and since he had never even seen it before, it held no sentimental value for him. Why leave him anything at all?

He turned the gun over, thumbed the cylinder release button on the left side of the frame. As the cylinder swung out, he saw that the gun was loaded. That was a damned foolish way to ship a weapon. It could have gone off if somebody had dropped that package. Hallam shook the cartridges from the chambers into the palm of his other hand.

Then he frowned, and his fingers closed slowly around the bullets. Something was wrong, and he was beginning to have an inkling of what it was.

———

HE SENT another wire to Chicago, advising his superiors at the Pinkerton Agency that he was unavailable for further assignments until he let them know otherwise. That would probably ruffle a few feathers, but Hallam didn't care. There was something else he had to do.

The next day, he stepped off an Atchison, Topeka &

Santa Fe Railroad car at the depot in Raton, New Mexico. Nestled between two arms of the rugged Sangre de Cristo Mountains, the town served the large ranches in the area and was also the last stop before the spectacular ascent of Raton Pass. The Colorado border was just on the other side of the pass.

Hallam walked through the railroad station and onto the main street of the town. The buildings along the street were made of either adobe or red brick. Raton was bustling, industrious. A few horseless carriages were parked along the street and one was even chugging along raising a cloud of dust, reminding Hallam that it was the Twentieth Century now. But the streets were still unpaved, and they knew a lot more wagon wheels and horses' hooves than they did hard rubber tires.

Though it was spring, the altitude was high enough so that the sheepskin jacket Hallam wore felt good against the chill in the air. He walked along the street, trying to remember from his last visit to Raton where Red Rosie's place had been. Following his instincts, he turned a corner into a cross street, and things started to look more familiar. He walked past a Spanish-style residence with a walled-in courtyard and red tiles on the roof, then came to a large frame structure with a long porch on its front. He went up the steps to the porch.

A large man was sitting in a straight-backed chair on the porch. He had the chair rocked back against the wall. Looking up at Hallam from under the brim of his hat, he said, "Howdy, hoss. Something I can do for you?"

"This is Rose Taggart's place, ain't it? I'm lookin' for her."

The man let the chair's front legs down with a thump. "Reckon you ain't heard the news, hoss. Miz Taggart's dead. This house belongs to Cap Baldwin now."

Hallam shook his head. "Never heard of him."

"Don't reckon there's any law says you have to've heard of him, but it's still his." The man jerked a thumb toward the door. "Go on in. Just 'cause there's been a change in ownership don't mean the gals won't treat you nice."

Hallam stayed where he was. "What happened to Mrs. Taggart?"

"I wouldn't know, hoss." The man tipped his chair back again, then reached inside his shirt pocket and took out the makin's. "Cap don't pay me to palaver. Go on in or don't, whatever you want. Suit yourself, hoss."

Hallam said, "My name's not hoss." He reached out with his right foot, hooked the toe of his boot under one of the chair legs, and jerked upward. The legs went out from under the chair and dumped its occupant on the porch with a crash. Tobacco from the pouch scattered around him.

The man came up off the porch with a roar of rage. He was big, no more than two inches shorter than Hallam and probably ten or fifteen pounds heavier. But his first punch was slow and looping, and Hallam had no trouble stepping inside it and slamming a hard right into the man's mouth. The man fell back against the wall behind him.

Hallam crowded him, hooking a left to the belly then bringing up a right that jerked the man's head back. Hallam caught hold of the man's shirt with both hands and turned, hauling the man around so that he crashed into and over the railing along the front of the porch. The man tumbled to the ground and landed so hard that all the breath was knocked out of him. He lay there pale and gasping, his mouth moving like that of a fish.

The commotion had attracted some attention inside, as Hallam figured it would. He turned back toward the front door as it was flung open. A tall, thick-set man with a shock of pale hair rushed onto the porch carrying a shotgun. Hallam stood still and kept his right hand well away from the butt of the Colt holstered on his hip. He didn't want to give the hombre with the scatter-gun an excuse to get trigger-happy.

"What the hell's goin' on out here?" the newcomer demanded in a heavily accented voice that Hallam pegged as coming from Arkansas. "Rooster, what're you doin' just layin' down there on the ground?"

The man Hallam had thrown off the porch sucked down some more air, then pointed a finger at him. "That son of a bitch done it!"

"Bein' called a name like that riles me even more than bein' called hoss," Hallam said.

The shotgunner lowered the double barrels of his weapon slightly. "Rooster, you been annoyin' the payin' customers again?"

"I never... He come up and started askin' questions."

"Questions about what?"

"About Rose Taggart," Hallam said. "I heard she owned this place, and that she and her girls sure knew how to show a man a good time."

"Oh." The shotgun went down even more. "Well,

then, hell, this is all just a misunderstandin'." The man tucked the Greener under his arm and stepped forward with his hand extended. "I'm Captain Patrick Henry Baldwin, the current owner of this establishment."

Hallam shook hands with him. "Name's Lucas."

"You just come right on inside, Lucas. The first drink is on the house, to make up for Rooster's boorish behavior. He just don't know how to act around quality folks, you understand?"

"Sure," Hallam said. He allowed Baldwin to draw him inside the building.

The place wasn't as opulent as some of the whorehouses Hallam had seen in his life, but it was well-furnished—in more ways than one. Crystal chandeliers lit the parlor, and their illumination was necessary because heavy red velvet drapes were drawn tight over the windows, shutting out the afternoon sun. The rug under Hallam's boots was thick. The walls were covered with fancy paper, and plushly upholstered armchairs and divans were scattered around the room. Several attractive young women in various stages of undress made use of the furniture, draping themselves over it in blatantly sensual poses. All of them smiled at Hallam and Baldwin as the two men came into the room.

Baldwin put a friendly hand on Hallam's arm and steered him across the parlor toward a bar. A man with a large bald spot on the back of his head stood behind the bar, polishing glasses. Baldwin said to him, "Quentin, a glass of our finest for Mr. Lucas here. On the house."

"Yes, sir." Quentin took a bottle from under the bar

and poured the drink. He looked at Baldwin and raised an eyebrow, and Baldwin indicated that he wanted a drink, too. Quentin splashed liquor into another glass.

Baldwin clinked his glass against Hallam's. "To your health, sir."

Hallam grunted an acknowledgement, then tossed back the drink. It was good whiskey that actually matched the label on the bottle, instead of the bathtub-brewed panther piss he'd halfway been expecting.

"What do you think?" Baldwin asked with a grin.

"Good," Hallam said.

"Nothing but the best for Cap Baldwin's customers," the man said, pride in his voice. He waved a hand toward the waiting women. "As you can see for yourself. Anything that pleases your fancy, Lucas?"

Hallam turned and ran his eyes over the women. Most of them were young, either in their teens or barely out of them. But one of them, a slender ash blonde who wore a short wrapper of white silk and stood behind a divan resting her hands on it, was older, probably in her late twenties. Hallam nodded toward her and said, "That lady right there."

"You're a man of refined tastes, sir," Baldwin said. "Angela, come over here."

The blonde came out from behind the divan. Her legs were long and clean and good. She smiled at Hallam and took his hand, said, "Hello."

Hallam nodded. "Ma'am."

"Angela, this is Lucas. You treat him right, you hear?"

"I certainly will."

Still holding his hand, she led him out of the parlor and up a staircase to the second floor. Close beside her like this, Hallam could smell her perfume. It smelled good. Instead of dousing herself in the stuff, the way most whores did, she had showed some restraint.

They reached the second floor landing and went along a balcony to a room with an open door. Several other doors off the balcony were closed. Angela took Hallam into the room, which was furnished with a bed, a porcelain chamber pot, a single chair, and a small table with a basin of water on it. She closed the door and turned back to face him, her hand going to the belt that was knotted around her waist, keeping the wrapper closed. "I'm glad you picked me, Lucas," she said.

Hallam's hand went out and touched her hands, stopping her from untying the belt. "Hold on," he said. "Do you remember me?"

Angela frowned a little. "Well, I thought you looked familiar when I first saw you downstairs. You're a big man. Have you been here before?"

"About two years ago was the last time."

"That was when Rose still—" Angela stopped short and stared at Hallam, her eyes widening. "Lucas," she said in a hushed voice. "Not... Lucas Hallam?"

He nodded.

And the cracks that were starting to show in her carefully controlled composure split wide open. Her face twisted and tears began to roll down her cheeks and she stepped forward into Hallam's arms, burying her face against his broad chest as she cried.

———

LATER, when Angela had calmed down a little, she and Hallam sat side by side on the edge of the bed and she said, "Nobody from the old days comes here anymore, Lucas. Even all the girls from that time are gone, except for me."

"Figured as much," Hallam said. "That's why I picked you downstairs. I thought maybe you could tell me what happened to Rose."

"Baldwin happened," Angela said, bitterness and anger in her voice. "He showed up in town and sweet-talked his way in here. He's a gambler, and Rose let him run a poker game here. You know some of the men like to play cards as well as... the other things they do here."

Hallam nodded.

"None of the girls liked him much," Angela went on. "He was rough with some of them. Never with me, but I heard about it from the others. I told them they ought to tell Rose, but we all knew how she felt about him, and they didn't want to hurt her."

"Seems like a lady as smart as Rose would've seen through a skunk like that."

"You'd think so. But you know how it is sometimes. You fall in love with somebody, and you convince yourself that all their flaws aren't really there."

Hallam supposed that was true. He'd had his heart broken a few times because he hadn't wanted to see certain things that he should have.

"Anyway, Rose started to get sick, and she relied more and more on Baldwin to run things around here. Finally, after about six months, she... she died."

"From what?" Hallam asked. "What sickness did she have?"

Angela shook her head. "The doctor never could figure it out for sure. Rose just wasted away to nothing, and then she was gone."

Hallam's jaw tightened. He didn't like to think about Rose like that. Vital, beautiful Rose, as full of life as any woman he'd ever known.

"How'd Baldwin get his hands on the house?"

"She left it to him in her will. That didn't really surprise any of us, but we didn't like it. One by one, the girls who were here then all drifted away, rather than stay on and work for him. All but me."

"Why didn't you leave, too?"

She laughed. "I'm too old, Lucas. I don't want to have to start over somewhere else. And Baldwin doesn't bother me very often. He prefers the younger girls. I have to put up with Rooster and Quentin, but..."

"You said Rose left the house to Baldwin in her will. Who handled that?"

"There's a lawyer here in Raton who was a customer. Still is, for that matter. He works for a law firm down in Santa Fe, but he's the one who drew up the will. His name is Arthur McKagen."

Hallam nodded. He knew the name from the letter he'd gotten in El Paso, along with the Ladysmith revolver.

"I need to have a talk with the fella. You say his office is here in town?"

"Just down the block from the train station. Lucas..." She laid a hand on his arm. "Why are you here?"

"Rose left me something in her will, too."

"I'm guessing you don't want me to tell Baldwin who you really are."

"Let's leave him in the dark a while longer," Hallam said.

Angela's hand went to the opening of the wrapper at her throat. "While we're here, do you want to..."

Hallam smiled. "Maybe when this is all over."

———

ARTHUR MCKAGEN WAS A SHORT, stocky man who looked impatient when Hallam came up to him on the sidewalk in front of the building where his office was located.

"I'm closed for the day," the lawyer said. "You'll have to come back tomorrow."

Hallam shook his head. "Sorry, I have to talk to you today. It's about Rose Taggart."

"Rose... I'm sorry, I can't discuss a client's business."

"I'm Lucas Hallam. I got a letter from you. And a package."

McKagen knew the name. "Hallam? I sent that letter nearly two months ago."

"It took a while to find me. I move around a lot."

"Well, Mr. Hallam, obviously you were acquainted with Mrs. Taggart, and for that reason I offer you my condolences on her passing. But I really have to get home to my wife—"

"Does she know that you were one of Red Rosie's *clients*?"

McKagen stopped short and glared at Hallam. "What you are implying, sir, is nothing less than blackmail!"

"All I need is a few minutes of your time. There're some things I got to get straightened out."

McKagen sighed and said, "Very well, come in. But only for a few minutes. My wife would probably be more upset if I were late for dinner than if she found out I, ah, patronized Mrs. Taggart's establishment on occasion."

The lawyer sat down behind his desk but didn't take off his hat. Neither did Hallam as he lowered himself into a red leather chair in front of the desk. "Tell me about Mrs. Taggart's will," he said.

McKagen shrugged. "There's nothing much to tell. The document went through probate and is now a matter of public record. Mrs. Taggart made a few small bequests to individuals, personal items for the most part, such as that gun she left to you, but the bulk of her estate, including her house, went to Captain Patrick H. Baldwin."

"Why would she leave practically everything to Baldwin?"

"I didn't ask her," McKagen said. "That wasn't really my business. But I suppose they were... close friends."

"But not married."

"No. However, an estate does not have to be left to a spouse. In this case, Mrs. Taggart was a widow and never remarried, so that would be impossible."

"What do you know about Baldwin?"

McKagen frowned. "Really, Mr. Hallam, this conversation is quite inappropriate."

"Be easier if you just answer my question, so your wife don't have to wait supper any longer than necessary."

"Very well, if you insist. But I don't know a great deal at all about Mr. Baldwin. He arrived in Raton about a year ago, claiming to be a cattle buyer. I don't think he ever bought any cattle, however. He spent most of his time at Mrs. Taggart's, playing cards, and eventually he spent all his time there."

"What about Rooster and Quentin? Did they come to Raton with him?"

"Who? Oh, you mean the two men who work there at the house. No, he hired them after Mrs. Taggart passed away. I don't recall seeing them around town before that."

But Baldwin could have sent for them, Hallam thought. He had gotten the feeling that Baldwin had known Rooster and Quentin for quite a while.

"Is there anything else?" McKagen asked.

Hallam thought about it, then shook his head. "No, I reckon not." He stood up.

Before Hallam reached the door, McKagen said, "You know, it's odd."

Hallam looked back. "What's odd?"

"You don't strike me as the type to be sentimental about a gun, Mr. Hallam. No offense, but you seem more the sort who would regard a weapon simply as a tool."

Hallam turned that comment over in his mind, then said, "Rose told you I was attached to that gun she left me, did she?"

"She said it carried a great deal of importance to you, as well as to her."

"Let me guess," Hallam said. "She came in and added that part of the will after the rest of it was already drawn up."

McKagen coughed. "Well, actually, I was at her place one evening when she asked me to come into her office. We drew up the codicil right there, and she gave me the wooden box with the gun inside it. I brought it back here that night."

"How long after that was it she died?"

"Only a week," McKagen said. "You almost missed out on your inheritance, such as it is, Mr. Hallam."

"Yeah," Hallam said. "Reckon I'm lucky."

———

HE HAD LEFT his warbag at the Santa Fe Railroad station. He picked it up, then walked over to the Raton House and got a room for the night. After eating supper in the hotel dining room, he went outside and took a deep breath of the cold night air.

It was time.

Hallam patted his coat, feeling the shape of the wooden box containing the Ladysmith revolver, which he had taken from his warbag and slipped into an inner pocket before eating.

"I'll square it, Rose," he muttered.

Rooster was still on the porch of the big house, but he wasn't sitting now. He stood there near the door with his arms folded, a glare on his beard-stubbled face as Hallam came up the steps.

"What're you doin' back here?" Rooster demanded.

"A fella gets an itch, he's got to scratch it," Hallam said.

Rooster mumbled something obscene. Hallam ignored him and walked inside.

Baldwin was in the parlor, leaning on the bar and talking in low tones with Quentin. The place was much busier now than it had been in the middle of the afternoon. Several men were sitting around sipping drinks and talking to the scantily clad women. Hallam saw Angela and gave her a brief nod, then went across the room to the bar.

"Well, Lucas, I didn't expect to see you back so soon," Baldwin greeted him. The man chuckled. "Angela must have made an impression on you."

"She sure did," Hallam said.

"She's yours for the takin', if you'd like."

Hallam shook his head. "I had something else in mind first. I've heard that you like to play a game of cards now and then."

Baldwin laughed. "Card playing is one of my vices, sure enough. My poor old Baptist mama tried to beat it out of me, but she never succeeded, rest her soul."

"Reckon we could get up a game?"

"I think that could be arranged." Baldwin looked around the room. "I see a few gents in attendance tonight who favor a game of cards when they get the chance. I'll speak to them, find out if they're interested. In the meantime, Quentin, why don't you show Lucas to the card room and give him a drink?"

"Sure thing, Cap," Quentin said.

Hallam followed the bartender into a small room that opened off the parlor. It contained a baize-covered poker table surrounded by chairs, as well as a small bar in one corner. Quentin set out glasses around the table and produced a bottle of whiskey. Hallam took a seat with his back to a blank wall, and Quentin filled the glass in front of him. He put the cork back in the bottle and set it in the middle of the table.

Baldwin came in with four other men, three of them dressed in town clothes and looking prosperous, the fourth man in the boots and jeans and Stetson of a cattleman. "Lucas, meet Ed Gloster," Baldwin said, indicating the rancher.

Hallam stood up and shook hands. "Howdy, Gloster."

"Lucas is the handle, is it?"

"That's right."

Hallam thought he saw something in Gloster's eyes, recognition, maybe. He wasn't personally acquainted with the cattleman, but Gloster could have seen him somewhere, might even know his real name. But if that was the case, Gloster was going to keep it to himself. He just nodded and sat down.

Baldwin introduced the other men to Hallam: Frank Randall, John Edwards, and Parley Barnett. "Parley's our mayor," Baldwin added.

The portly Barnett looked embarrassed. "Now, we don't need to be goin' on about things like that," he said. "I'm sure Mr. Lucas ain't interested in local politics."

"I've heard it said that when you come right down to it, all politics is local," Hallam said. "Me, I never paid much attention to such things."

"That's probably wise," Frank Randall said with a chuckle. "There are a lot more important things in life. Like poker."

Baldwin took a seat and began unwrapping a new deck of cards. "Spoken like a true card player, Frank," he said.

The game got underway. Hallam tilted his hat back on his head and concentrated on his cards. For the first few hands, the players were feeling each other out, although these locals probably had played together before and knew each other's habits. But Hallam was a stranger, and therefore something of a wild card.

Baldwin was a good player, and as far as Hallam could tell, he wasn't cheating. The pile of bills and coins in front of him grew steadily as the game progressed. He wasn't winning so much, though, as to offend the other men. That, as much as anything, was proof of his skill.

Hallam didn't have a lot of cash on him, but that was just as well. He didn't want to prolong this. When one of the pots began to grow, he stayed in when he might have dropped out otherwise. So did Baldwin, raising consistently. One by one, the other players folded as they sensed that something was developing between Hallam and Baldwin. When the bet came to him, Hallam saw it and raised, using the last of his money. Baldwin's expression had grown more intense. The competitive juices were flowing in him, Hallam knew. Baldwin smiled and said, "Well, Lucas, I'm just going to have to see that bet and bump it up a little more. I have faith in my cards."

Hallam glanced at his cards without really seeing them. He didn't give a damn whether he won the hand or not. All he'd been doing was leading up to this moment.

"Are you going to call?" Baldwin prodded.

"I'll do more than that," Hallam said. He laid his cards face down on the table in front of him and reached inside his coat. "I'll cover the bet and raise it." He brought out the polished wooden box and placed it on the table.

"What's that?" Mayor Barnett asked.

Baldwin's eyes narrowed to slits as he looked at the box. Hallam didn't know if he recognized it or not, but his instincts must have kicked in, warning him that something unusual was going on.

Hallam unfastened the catch and opened the lid of

the box. "I figure this is worth enough, especially to you, Baldwin."

Ed Gloster leaned forward and looked at the gun lying in its bed of red velvet. "I've seen pistols like that before," he said. "It's called a Ladysmith, isn't it?"

"That's right," Hallam said. "It's a Smith & Wesson, .22 caliber."

Baldwin licked his lips. "That's a nice little gun, Lucas, but it's not hardly worth enough— ".

"Oh, it's not the gun itself," Hallam said. "What I'm really bettin' are the bullets."

"The bullets?" Randall said. "How can bullets be worth anything?"

Hallam took the Ladysmith out of the box and opened the cylinder, turning the gun so that the men around the table could see that it was fully loaded. "This is the way the gun came to me," he said. "I inherited it from Rose Taggart."

"Red Rosie?" Gloster exclaimed. "You knew her?"

Hallam nodded, his eyes fixed on Baldwin now. "I did. Not as well as I might've liked, but we were pretty close."

Baldwin's pose of affability had vanished now. "I don't know what you're doin' here, but this game is over."

"Not until we finish this hand," Hallam said. He shook the bullets out into his palm. "I understand why you might not want to let me bet the gun, but these cartridges are mighty valuable."

He brought one of them to his mouth and bit the lead bullet, pulling it loose from the shell. Hallam spit out the bullet, then turned the shell upside down so that a tiny, tightly rolled piece of paper fell out of it.

"Every one of these cartridges has a message inside it, Baldwin," Hallam went on. "They're in Rose Taggart's handwriting. I reckon there are people here in Raton who'll recognize it without any trouble. They tell the whole story of how you came here and fooled her into thinking you loved her, while all the time you planned to kill her and take over her place. She even found the poison you'd been feedin' to her in small doses for months, makin' her sicker and sicker. But by then it was too late, and she knew it. She knew she was goin' to die. All she could do was leave behind a last request. So she left me this gun, and these bullets, knowin' I'd settle the score for her."

The room was completely silent as Hallam finished talking. Several heartbeats went by with Baldwin staring across the table at Hallam. Then Ed Gloster said, "Can I see that?"

Hallam handed him the note he had taken from the opened cartridge. Gloster unrolled it, looked at the words written on it, and said, "That's Rose's hand, all right." He looked up at Hallam. "I know you now, Hallam. I was up in Pueblo a few years back when you caught up with the Wilson brothers. How did Rose know you'd look inside these bullets?"

"She knew I wouldn't leave a gun sitting around loaded like that when it wasn't going to be used," Hallam said. "And I reckon she was counting on the fact that I could tell something was wrong with them, just by the weight and feel of them."

"That was a risky bet."

"The way Baldwin kept her cooped up here in the house all the time, it was the only way she had to get in touch with me. She didn't want him to know she was on to what he was doin' to her." Hallam's mouth curved in a cold, humorless smile. "I reckon she wanted it to be a surprise when I came to see Baldwin."

"You can't prove any of this," Baldwin said, his voice hollow.

Hallam's left hand brushed the bullets, sent them rolling into the center of the table. "We've got Rose's own words to prove it," he said. "So how about it, Baldwin? Are you goin' to call the bet or not?"

Baldwin moved, his left arm coming up under the table and upsetting it while he surged to his feet and grabbed under his coat for a gun with his right hand. Hallam fell backward in his chair, away from the table, and the other four men dived for the corners of the room, getting as far out of the line of fire as they could. The revolver that appeared in Baldwin's hand blasted twice, but Hallam was already rolling to the side. As he came up on one knee, the Colt on his hip seemed to leap into his hand. He fired once, driving a slug into Baldwin's chest. Baldwin was thrown back against the wall behind him, but he stayed on his feet and tried to raise his gun for another shot. Hallam triggered again, and this time when Baldwin hit the wall, he bounced off and fell forward on his face.

The door into the card room burst open, and Quentin tried to bring a sawed-off shotgun to bear on Hallam. Off to the side, another pistol barked. Quentin jerked around, dropping the scattergun and clutching at his shoulder where a bullet had drilled it. Hallam looked over and saw Ed Gloster holding a gun. He nodded and said, "Much obliged."

The cattleman grunted. "Rose Taggart was my friend, too," he said.

The shots had set off quite a commotion elsewhere in the house. Men were shouting questions and curses, and somewhere a woman screamed in fear. Rooster's big figure suddenly loomed in the doorway of the card room, but he stopped in his tracks as he found himself facing the guns held by Hallam and Gloster.

"Your horse out back, Rooster?" Gloster asked.

"Uh, yeah." Rooster's stunned gaze was fastened on Baldwin's crumpled body.

"Well, then, if I was you, I'd saddle up and ride out of Raton, right now. And I wouldn't ever come back." Gloster glanced over at Hallam. "That all right with you?"

Hallam nodded. Rooster had probably known what Baldwin was doing to Rose Taggart, and a part of him wanted to kill the son of a bitch, but Baldwin was dead and Hallam supposed that was enough.

Rooster backed out of the room, then turned tail and ran. Hallam holstered his Colt and looked down at the wounded Quentin. "When he's been patched up, I reckon he ought to leave, too."

Gloster nodded. "We'll see to it." He looked around at the other men. "We'll make things right for Red Rosie, won't we, boys?"

The townsmen muttered their agreement. Chances were, they would hush up the whole thing, Hallam thought, especially the mayor. But he didn't care. Rose's death had been avenged, and that was all that mattered.

That, and one more thing.

"There's a lady who works here named Angela," Hallam said. "I reckon the place ought to go to her now. That lawyer, McKagen, can likely fix it up all legal-like."

"Sure," Gloster said. "What about you, Hallam?"

Hallam scooped up the cartridges, thumbed them back into the cylinder of the Ladysmith. He closed it, put the gun in the wooden box, and lowered the lid. "There's a train out of here in the morning," he said as he put the box in his coat. "Reckon I'll be on it."

HOLLYWOOD FLESH

As a hard-headed old cowboy, Lucas Hallam doesn't believe in zombies. But in Hollywood Flesh, his most recent case is starting to give him nightmares...

"WHAT THE HELL IS A ZOMBIE?" asked Lucas Hallam.

Martin Larribee puffed on his pipe for a moment before answering. "One of the walking dead. One who has risen from the grave to shamble about in a grotesque, twisted mockery of life."

Hallam thought about that. If he hadn't already known that Larribee was a writer, he would have been able to tell it from the way the Englishman talked. Finally, he shook his head and said, "Nothin' dead can get up and walk around again. It ain't natural."

From where she sat in a comfortable armchair near the fireplace on the other side of the crowded living room in Larribee's Hollywood apartment, Eliza Dutton laughed. "Now you understand, Mr. Hallam. It certainly isn't natural."

She and Larribee made a pretty odd pair. The Englishman was short and stocky, with sandy hair and a drooping mustache. Eliza Dutton was tall and slender and darkly beautiful. Hallam had seen her around ever since she'd arrived in town a few years earlier, in '25. Her name then had been Gertrude Something-or-other. Hallam had never heard anything else about her background. But she had gone from bit parts to ingénues to second leads in a hurry, and now she had a couple of leading roles to her credit.

Hallam rubbed his jaw, feeling the two days' worth of stubble. Since he'd known he would be working today, he hadn't bothered to shave this morning. "I just don't know if I can do you any good, Mr. Larribee."

"Because you don't believe that zombies exist? Look at yourself, Mr. Hallam. Aren't you a creature of myth?"

Hallam glanced down at his outfit. It was true that not many folks wore fringed buckskins these days, or packed a long-barreled Colt .45 in a tied-down holster, along with a sheathed Bowie knife on the other hip, or looked at the world from under the broad brim of a high-crowned brown Stetson. But there was nothing mythological about any of it. The costume department at the studio didn't have to come up with anything for him to wear when he was working on a picture. These duds were the real thing. He'd owned them for years.

"Cowboys are real," he said. "I reckon I'll have to take your word on it for zombies, Mr. Larribee, 'cause I ain't never seen one. Hope I never do."

Larribee took his pipe out of his mouth and wearily scrubbed a hand over his face. "I wish I could say the same about never seeing one, I honestly wish I could. But I have seen them, Mr. Hallam. I know they exist." The Englishman raised his head and met Hallam's eyes squarely. "I know because they want to kill me and eat my flesh."

Yep, thought Hallam, this fella has definitely been into the loco weed.

Larribee put out a hand. There was a hint of desperation in his manner. "Please, Mr. Hallam, hear me out. I know that you sometimes work as a... a private inquiry agent—"

"Private detective."

"Yes, of course. A private detective. And to put it in simple terms, someone is trying to kill me. I want you to put a stop to it."

"If somebody's been threatenin' you, go to the police."

"And tell them what?" Larribee shrugged helplessly. "I saw how you reacted a moment ago. Do you honestly believe the authorities would give any credence to my story or try to help me if I told them the same thing?"

Hallam thought about the detectives he knew on the police forces in Hollywood and Los Angeles. "They'd think you were off your nut."

"Precisely. That's why I need to hire you to act on my behalf."

Hallam was holding his hat in his left hand. He tapped it against his leg as he thought. He was tired from riding all over Bronson Canyon all day, pretending to be one of the outlaw gang that Ken Maynard was after, but he didn't suppose it would hurt anything to listen to what Larribee had to say.

"All right, you can tell me about it. I ain't promisin' I'll take the case, though."

"Fair enough. Please sit down."

Hallam lowered his rangy, powerful frame into an armchair and waited.

Larribee drew up a chair near the unlit fireplace, next to Eliza Dutton. "I'm a scenarist, as I told you when I called. Perhaps you're familiar with my work?"

Writers, thought Hallam. "Can't say as I pay much attention to the names on the scripts when I read 'em."

"Yes, well, no matter. I've published several novels in England, and I came to America several years ago to try my luck over here. Done quite well, if I say so myself. I've written features for some of the leading studios."

And been paid pretty well for it, Hallam decided as he looked around the expensively furnished apartment. Larribee had himself a good-looking actress as a lady-friend, too, and that cost money.

Larribee puffed on his pipe. "Well, to the point of the matter. A couple of months ago, I went to Haiti to research a scenario. Geoffrey Mason planned to make a picture about the sugar cane plantations on Hispaniola, and he wanted me to write it for him."

Hallam nodded. He knew Mason, another Englishman who'd had some success as a producer and director after coming to Hollywood in the early '20s.

"Geoffrey went along on the trip to search for suitable locations, and so did Eliza here, who was scheduled to play the female lead."

That jogged something in Hallam's brain. As a rule, he didn't pay much attention to the gossip columns in the trades, but he recalled seeing some mention of Eliza

Dutton and Geoffrey Mason being engaged. Now Eliza was in Martin Larribee's apartment, and seeing as how she was wearing a silk dressing gown and not a hell of a lot else, she obviously wasn't planning on going home tonight. Larribee had done more in Haiti than research.

Larribee took a deep breath. "While we were there, Eliza and I... well, we fell in love, Mr. Hallam. I'll not deny it."

"Neither will I," Eliza said softly.

"Naturally, Geoffrey wasn't pleased with this, but we're all professionals, after all. We continued with the work that had taken us to that lovely but haunted island. Geoffrey told me that he had found a perfect spot to film the picture, an old deserted plantation house out in the forest northeast of Port-au-Prince. He suggested that I go out and take a look at it, that it might... inspire me in my writing. I agreed to do so."

"But it was some sort of double-cross," said Hallam.

"He told me to go at dusk." Larribee seemed not to have heard Hallam's comment. "He said the light was spectacular then. That much was true. With the sun setting over the sea to the west, and the golden light washing over that old, moss-draped plantation house, surrounded by trees and with the green mountains and the darkening eastern sky behind it... it truly was a beautiful scene."

Hallam could see it clearly. Larribee was a pretty fair word wrangler.

"But that wasn't all that was there. I walked right in on the... the most ghastly thing...."

Larribee stopped, and Eliza Dutton leaned forward in her chair, reaching over to him to rest a hand on his arm. After a moment, the Englishman was able to go on.

"I had walked into a voodoo ritual. Do you know what voodoo is, Mr. Hallam?"

"I ain't rightly sure."

"The actual name is *voudon*. It's the old religion of the former slaves and their descendants, brought with them from Africa. A dark religion, Mr. Hallam, full of vengeful gods and bloody sacrifices."

"And dead fellers who get up and walk around when they take a notion to," Hallam guessed.

Larribee nodded. "That's right. The voodoo priests, called *houngans*, can recall the dead to life as zombies. They rise from the grave, unthinking monsters who obey only the will of the houngan, filled with an unholy craving for... for human flesh."

Hallam leaned forward. "You saw this?"

"God help me, I did. The ritual I interrupted involved the raising of a new zombie. And just as I came along, the... the thing was given a young Haitian woman—" Larribee's pipe rattled on the floor as he dropped it and pressed his hands over his face. "My God, I wish I could get that awful sight out of my mind! That woman's screams still echo in my ears. I screamed, too. I couldn't help it. But that drew the attention of the voodoo worshipers to me. An outsider. A white man. Having witnessed their blasphemous practices, I couldn't be allowed to live. They pursued me."

Larribee lowered his hands and looked across the room at Hallam again. "I ran faster than I ever have in my life, Mr. Hallam. Thank God the car I had rented started quickly and easily. I was able to drive away from there before they caught me. I returned to Port-au-Prince and told Geoffrey and Eliza that I had to leave right away and come back here to California. I pleaded a sudden illness. Eliza agreed to come with me."

"What about Mason?"

"He was angry, of course. He said it was because I was running out on his picture. But he was really angry because his attempt to murder me had failed."

"Murder?"

"Of course. Somehow, Geoffrey found out about the ritual that would be going on at that plantation, and he sent me out there so I would stumble on it and be killed. That was his way of eliminating me so that he could try to win back Eliza's affections."

Hallam looked at Eliza Dutton. "When did he tell you about all this?"

"On the airplane back here."

"And you believe him?"

Eliza took Larribee's hand. "Of course. Martin wouldn't lie."

Hallam thought about it. Maybe Eliza Dutton was just being loyal to Larribee, or maybe she was as loco as he was.

"Where's Mason now?"

"Back here in Hollywood," Larribee said. "He took a later flight. He's abandoned the Haitian picture, at least for now."

Hallam put his hands on his knees, ready to push himself to his feet and get out of there. "I reckon what you'd best do is not go to any of the same parties as Mason does until he gets over bein' mad at you. No charge for the advice."

Quickly, Larribee put out his hands. "No, Mr. Hallam, you don't understand. Geoffrey's not the only one who came back here from Haiti. He brought the houngan—and a zombie—with him. You see, once an interloper has witnessed one of their rituals, these voodoo worshipers will track him down to the ends of the earth to kill him. That's the only way to satisfy what they see as an affront to their gods."

Hallam leaned back in his chair. "You mean there's one o' these voodoos—I mean, zombies—chasin' you around Hollywood tryin' to kill you and eat you?"

"I know it sounds insane! But I swear it's the truth. I swear it on all that's still holy in a world grown ever darker and more evil."

Eliza Dutton said, "It is the truth, Mr. Hallam. I've seen the Haitian man—the priest—and his... creature stalking Martin. One night he barely escaped from them. You have to help us."

Hallam sighed. He had never been good at turning down folks who were in trouble. While he didn't believe everything Larribee had told him, it was possible that as a jilted lover, Geoffrey Mason was doing *something* to scare the bejabbers out of his fellow Englishman.

"I reckon I can look into it, but I ain't makin' no promises."

Instantly, Larribee was out of his chair and across the room, shaking Hallam's hand. "Thank you, Mr. Hallam, thank you. I've spoken to quite a few people in the motion picture community, and they assure me that you're quite a competent fellow. And discreet as well. That's very important."

Sure it is, thought Hallam, *because if word gets out that you're crazy as a loon, you might have trouble getting work.*

On the other hand, this is Hollywood.

———

LUCAS HALLAM HAD BEEN a lot of things in his time: Texas Ranger, Pinkerton operative, deputy United States marshal. Now in his fifties, he spent most of his days working as a riding extra and occasional stuntman in the countless Western pictures the studios cranked out. He liked the cowboys who worked in the movies with him. Most of them were the genuine article, fellas who had drifted to Hollywood because there wasn't enough real ranch work to go around in these modern times.

But Hallam was also a licensed private investigator and supplemented his picture income by taking a case now and then, usually one that had some connection to the studios or movie folks. Like Martin Larribee's. The next morning, as Hallam drove his battered old flivver through the main gate of the studio where Geoffrey Mason worked, he thought with a grin that maybe once this case was over, he could add zombie wrangler to his list of jobs.

The guard at the gate waved him through; Hallam knew every studio guard in Hollywood. He drove past several huge soundstage buildings to park in front of a row of neat little bungalows that served as production offices.

A secretary at a desk in the front room of one of the bungalows looked up as Hallam came in. "I'd like to see Mr. Mason," Hallam said.

He wasn't wearing buckskins and a Stetson today. Instead he wore a dark brown suit and a cream-colored Panama hat. He still carried the same .45, however, tucked into a holster under his left arm. The sheath that held the Bowie knife hung between his shoulder blades from a thong around his neck.

"I don't believe you have an appointment, Mr....?"

"Hallam. Tell him it's about Haiti."

Hallam had noticed that the door into the other room was open. He spoke loudly enough to be heard in there, and sure enough, a second later, a man poked his head out. "Haiti? What the devil?"

Hallam recognized Geoffrey Mason. They had never been introduced, but Hallam had seen him around town. Ignoring the disapproving look the secretary gave him, he stepped toward the door and extended his hand. "Lucas Hallam, Mr. Mason."

"How do you do." Mason shook Hallam's hand. "What's this about Haiti?"

"I hear you had some trouble with a picture you wanted to make down there. I'd like to talk to you about it."

Mason hesitated, then jerked his head toward the inner office. "Come in. No calls, Doris."

The secretary sniffed and nodded. Hallam stepped into the office, and Mason closed the door behind him.

The place wasn't fancy, just functional. The only touch of luxury was a small bar where bootleg booze could be dispensed. Successful producer-directors like Geoffrey Mason didn't have to go to a speakeasy to get their hooch.

Mason was slender and handsome, with sleek dark hair. He looked a lot more like the type to date beautiful actresses than Martin Larribee did. But Eliza Dutton was lounging around in silk dressing gowns in Larribee's apartment these days, not in Mason's Beverly Hills mansion.

Mason walked behind his desk. "What can I do for you, Mr.... Hallam, was it?"

"Martin Larribee says you sicced some voodoo priest on him down yonder in Haiti, and that now there's a zombie here in Hollywood that's tryin' to kill him." Sometimes when you slapped all your cards face-up on the table right away, it startled a gent into saying something he didn't want to.

Mason's eyes widened. "I say! That's mad!"

Hallam stayed on his feet but dropped his Panama on a chair in front of the desk. "Maybe so, but somethin's got him spooked, and since he took your gal away from you, I reckon you might have somethin' to do with it."

Mason's face darkened with anger. "So that's it. It's not enough that that miserable little scribbler stole Eliza away from me, now he's started spreading ugly rumors about me as well. Well, I won't stand for it, Mr. Hallam. I simply won't stand for it." His hand started toward a button on the desk. "I see this for what it is. You and Larribee intend to blackmail me. Go ahead and try. You'll be laughed out of Hollywood, and I'll sue both of you. But right now, if you don't leave immediately, I'll have you arrested for trespassing—"

Hallam leaned over the desk. His big hand covered the button without pressing it. "I ain't a blackmailer, Mason, and neither is Larribee. He just wants whatever's been goin' on to stop."

"The only thing going on is that Larribee has lost his mind!"

Hallam's eyes narrowed as he looked across the desk at Mason. He had survived a lot of years in an assortment of dangerous professions by being able to know when people were telling the truth. He had a feeling that Mason wasn't lying.

Hallam straightened and took his hand off the button. "You want to push that, go ahead. But it'll be ugly for you, too."

Abruptly, Mason sank into the leather chair behind the desk. "Just go away, Mr. Hallam. I don't want any trouble. I've had enough problems recently, what with having to postpone a picture because my leading lady and my scenarist walked out on me. I can replace them both, but the delay has cost a great deal of money."

"I reckon it's easier to replace a writer than a fiancee."

Mason laughed hollowly. "Not at all. This is Hollywood, after all. There's no shortage of beautiful young women eager to have a career in motion pictures. If not for those blasted morals clauses, think what a hotbed of debauchery this town would be."

"I reckon I'd rather not." Hallam picked up his hat. "Larribee better not have any more trouble, or I'll be back to see you, Mason."

Mason waved a hand. "Threaten me to your heart's content. I've done nothing to Larribee, nor do I intend to. That's a closed chapter in my life." He chuckled. "Larribee certainly has come up with a colorful story, though. Just imagine... zombies in Hollywood. The living dead stalking through the hills of Bel-Air..." Mason began to frown in thought. "Hmmm... there might be a picture in that."

Hallam tried not to grimace as he turned and walked out.

———

THE ONLY THING Hallam's visit to the studio had accomplished was to convince him that Geoffrey Mason wasn't responsible for whatever was happening to Martin Larribee. Mason hadn't seemed all that broken up about losing Eliza Dutton, either, so the idea that he had sent Larribee out in that plantation knowing he would interrupt a voodoo ritual and be marked for death was pretty far-fetched, too. Hallam supposed it could have happened that way, but he sensed that something else was going on here.

He still didn't believe in zombies, but something sure had Larribee spooked. Maybe the thing to do was keep an eye on the little Englishman for a few days and see if somebody tried to murder him.

Hallam figured zombies wouldn't wander around in broad daylight, not even in Hollywood, so he waited until that evening to go back over to Larribee's apartment. He had just parked the flivver and gotten out when he saw a figure running through the shadows toward him. Hallam's hand started under his coat toward the butt of his gun, but he paused as he heard Larribee's voice.

"Mr. Hallam! Thank God you're here! Eliza is in trouble."

"Hold on there," Hallam said as Larribee came up to him, panting from fear or exertion or both. "What are you talkin' about?"

"E-Eliza just called me. She said she saw the zombie when she was on her way over here earlier tonight. She tried to run it down with her car, but it escaped. But she followed the creature! She trailed it back to its lair!"

Hallam frowned. The story bubbling out of Larribee's mouth sounded like something a writer would come up with, not an actress. But whether Eliza Dutton was chasing a zombie or something else around town, she could still wind up in trouble.

"Did she say where she was?"

Larribee swallowed and nodded. "At an old house up off of Mulholland, near the Hollywoodland sign. Actually, she was calling from a drugstore at the bottom of the hill, but she said that was where the zombie went!"

Hallam tugged at his earlobe. "Wait a minute. I got the feelin' these zombies ain't supposed to be very fast on their feet. How'd the thing get all the way up there?"

"The houngan has a car. The creature got back to the vehicle, and it sped away. Eliza was able to follow it."

So now voodoo priests and zombies are driving around Hollywood, thought Hallam. *Well, California does have a way of changin' folks....*

He nodded abruptly, suddenly anxious to see just what Eliza Dutton had followed up into the hills. "Let's go."

"Really? You'll go with me?"

"Damn right. Pile into my flivver."

Larribee climbed eagerly into Hallam's car. Hallam drove through the streets of Hollywood, then started the climb up Mulholland onto the long, rugged ridge that overlooked the city. One of his cases had ended in a shootout up there near the Hollywoodland sign. He hoped that wouldn't happen tonight, but if it did, his Colt had five rounds in the cylinder and the hammer resting on an empty chamber.

Five was usually plenty when Lucas Hallam slapped leather.

Eliza Dutton had given Larribee good directions. "Right there!" he said excitedly when the flivver's headlights picked out a small dirt road turning off to the left. Hallam swung onto the winding road and followed it for about a quarter of a mile before they came to a large clearing where an old house stood. Beyond the house, the ground fell away and the lights of Los Angeles spread out across the valley in a glittering carpet.

Larribee let out a moan when he saw the old house. "It's like the one in Haiti!"

Hallam had never been to Haiti, but he figured the plantation houses there didn't look much like deserted old mansions in the Hollywood Hills. Still, the resemblance was close enough to put a scare into Larribee. The Englishman pressed back against the car seat.

"I don't know if I can do this."

"There's a car parked over there." Hallam pointed through the windshield. "Is it Miss Dutton's?"

"Oh, my God. Yes, that's Eliza's car. I have to find her. You don't think she went... in there?"

Hallam opened the door beside him. "Reckon we'd better find out."

He stepped out of the flivver. Larribee emerged tentatively from the other door. No sooner had they started walking toward the house than a scream rang out.

"Eliza!" Larribee shouted. He broke into a run, his fear momentarily forgotten.

Hallam went after him, the bad knee he had suffered years earlier when a horse fell on him slowing him slightly. Larribee reached the rotting old steps first and started up onto the porch.

A huge, slow-moving figure loomed out of the darkness and lurched into Larribee's path. Larribee's shriek of terror was cut short when a hand closed around his throat. As Hallam started up the steps, he saw moonlight shining on the gaunt, gray, hideous face of the thing that had hold of Larribee. The Englishman's wildly kicking feet came up off the porch as the creature lifted him by the neck.

"Drop him, you son of a bitch!"

Hallam didn't draw his gun. He went up the steps two at a time and lunged onto the porch. The zombie said, "Shit!" and swung Larribee around so that the Englishman was between it and Hallam. A hard shove sent Larribee reeling into the detective.

Hallam batted Larribee out of the way, figuring he could apologize to his client later for knocking him down, and caught hold of the zombie's shoulder as the creature turned to run. Hallam hauled the thing around and swung a hard right fist, landing the punch squarely on the zombie's jaw. The creature sailed back into the porch rail, broke through the rotten wood, and crashed down into what had once been a flowerbed.

"Be careful!" Larribee cried from where he lay on the porch. "The walking dead cannot feel pain! The only way to stop one is to cut off its head!"

The zombie groaned.

"Oh, I don't reckon we'll have to go cuttin' off any heads tonight," said Hallam. He reached for his gun. "But I do plan to keep this fella covered until we find out what's goin' on here."

Eliza Dutton spoke from the shadows at the other end of the porch. "Don't, Mr. Hallam." She came forward into the moonlight. It shone on the pistol in her hand.

The zombie in the flowerbed rolled onto its side and started cursing. It sat up and rubbed its jaw, then asked angrily, "What the hell did you hit me with, a two-by-four?"

Hallam ignored the creature and kept his eyes on Eliza Dutton, figuring she was the greater threat at the moment. "Where's the houngan?" he asked as he took his hand away from his gun.

Another figure came scurrying around the corner of the house and hurried over to the zombie. "Casey, you all right?" the newcomer asked worriedly.

"Yeah, Al," replied the zombie. "That big son of a bitch walloped me, that's all. Hey, lady, you said all we had to do was kill one little guy. Where'd this other jazzbo come from?"

"Will you two shut up?" Eliza grated. "Obviously, things didn't work out as planned."

Martin Larribee was still sitting on the porch. "E-Eliza?" He sounded stunned. "What are you doing?"

Eliza Dutton sighed. "Getting rid of you, Martin. And don't act so surprised. You blackmailed me into your bed, after all. My God, I was engaged to Geoffrey Mason! I would have played the lead in all of his pictures from now on!"

"But I... I thought you'd come to love me."

"A writer? Please, Martin, be reasonable."

Hallam had pieced some of it together on the drive up here, and now he thought he had the rest of it figured out. "You got Mason to suggest that Larribee go out to the old plantation house, didn't you, ma'am? Did you pay some fellas to pretend to put on a voodoo ritual?"

"No, that was real," Eliza said as she came a step

closer. The gun in her hand never wavered. "I heard about it from one of the maids in the hotel who was as impressed by the gods of Hollywood as she was by the gods of voodoo. I had learned enough about how seriously they take all that nonsense that I thought there was a good chance Martin wouldn't come back alive."

"But when he did, you got the idea to get rid of him once the two of you came back here."

"Imaginative people are easily frightened. I toyed with the idea of trying to actually scare him to death." Eliza shrugged. "But that was going to take too long."

Hallam jerked a thumb at the fake zombie and houngan. "So you decided to just have these two knock him off. You must not have liked it much when he called me."

"You were an annoyance, Mr. Hallam. But if you hadn't happened to come along tonight, everything would have been fine. Martin would have been dead—after having been made to suffer like I've suffered—and his death would have been blamed on zombies... or on Geoffrey."

"Would've made it hard for you to go back to Mason if he was under suspicion of murder."

"There are other producers in Hollywood."

Hallam knew she was right about that. Everything was easily replaceable in Hollywood, especially when you didn't have to worry about morals or honor or anything of the sort.

"What did Larribee have on you, anyway? I reckon it must've been something pretty bad if the studio could use it to break your contract."

"The little bastard found out somehow that

Gertrude Singleton is still wanted on prostitution and narcotics charges back in Illinois."

The only reason she's telling me this, thought Hallam, *is that she doesn't plan on me leaving here alive. And those two fools she hired to help her will die, too, more than likely. A clean sweep, and she's in the clear, ready to move on to the next important man who can help her career, now that her detour into Larribee's bed is over.*

"You know, as cool as you are about this, ma'am, I'd bet you've pulled the trigger a few times before."

"The less said about that, the better," Eliza noted.

The barrel of the gun in her hand came up slightly, and Hallam knew she was going to fire. He tensed, ready to try a leap to one side and a desperate grab for his own gun.

"Damn!" exclaimed the zombie. "What the hell is that?"

Eliza hesitated and turned her head. Hallam knew he ought to reach for his gun, but instead something made him look, too, and he saw the same thing the others had. Martin Larribee pushed himself back against the wall of the house and screamed.

Things were coming out of the woods around the clearing where the old house sat. Things that walked slowly and awkwardly, not like men but like creatures that had once been men.

The night breeze carried a foul scent to Hallam's nose. It smelled for all the world like rotten meat. He heard something that sounded like the beating of a drum, but it might have been the pounding of his own heart.

"What the hell?" said Eliza Dutton.

Hallam counted six of the things spread out in a half-circle. At first he had thought this might be another of Eliza's vicious tricks, but she sounded just as startled and frightened as Larribee was.

"Let's get out of here!"

That was Casey, the fake zombie. He and the other man, who had masqueraded as a houngan to frighten Larribee, ran toward the woods, trying to dart past the shambling figures. With shocking swiftness, two of the creatures lurched into their path and intercepted them. Casey was a big man, bigger than the thing that had hold of him, but it jerked him into the air as if he were a child. Casey screamed as bones began to crack in his body.

The other man didn't cry out at all. He couldn't. Bony fingers were locked around his throat, stifling any sound.

Hallam wasn't worried about Eliza Dutton anymore. He palmed out the Colt and brought it up. He'd seen gents who were hopped up before, and he figured that's what he was looking at now. But he'd never seen anything that couldn't be brought down with enough lead. There was plenty of moonlight for him to aim by as he squeezed off two shots.

Both slugs went through the right knee of the nearest creature. It fell as that leg collapsed underneath it.

But then it got back up again, seemingly without feeling any pain. Balancing awkwardly on its one good leg, it started toward the house again.

Hallam's jaw tightened, and he muttered, "Damn." He shot the other leg out from under the thing.

"The head!" screamed Martin Larribee. "You have to cut off the head!"

Sure enough, the creature Hallam had wounded kept coming, pulling itself along the ground with its arms.

Hallam reached into his coat pocket with one hand while he flipped open the Colt's cylinder with the other and dumped the empty shells. He thumbed fresh cartridges into the gun, loading all six chambers this time.

He had faced down owlhoots all over the West. This was no different, he told himself. A fella just had to keep a cool head....

Hallam brought up the Colt and blasted six slugs through the skull of the closest creature. That pretty much took its whole head off. It managed another step or two, then pitched to the ground and scrabbled around a little before finally growing still.

Hallam was already reloading again, trying to calculate mentally how many shells he had and how many it was going to take to fight off the... the...

Oh, hell, he thought, *might as well call the critters zombies.*

Eliza was firing at another of the creatures, but her aim wasn't as good as Hallam's. She hit it in the head a couple of times, but that didn't slow it down. The zombie reached the edge of the porch and threw itself toward her, breaking through the rotten railing and getting its hands on her. She shrieked and fought frantically, but the zombie was too strong for her by far.

"Let go of her!" howled Martin Larribee. Suddenly he was on his feet, throwing himself at Eliza and the creature that had hold of her. He battered it with his fists, but it swatted him aside. The zombie jerked Eliza's forearm upward and clamped his mouth on it, tearing out a ragged chunk of flesh as she screamed and spasmed.

Hallam tossed the Colt from his right hand to his left—the old border shift—then yanked the Bowie knife from the sheath at the back of his neck. He swung it with all his strength at the zombie. The razor-sharp blade sliced through rotting flesh, grated on bone, and then the zombie's head toppled off its shoulders. The thing collapsed, and so did Eliza.

Hallam swung around, saw that Martin Larribee was lying huddled against the house, either dead or unconscious. The detective drove the point of the Bowie into the wall so that it stayed there, quivering, within easy reach if he needed it. He pivoted, saw that another of the creatures was almost at the porch, and fired left-handed. The thing's head exploded, making the stink in the air even worse, and it went down.

Three of them were done for. The one with the legs shot out from under it finally made it to the porch and started pulling itself up the steps. Hallam took a step and swung his leg, and the toe of his boot caught the zombie under the chin. He hoped the thing's bones were brittle. The kick drove the zombie's head back. There was a sharp cracking and ripping sound, and the head came completely off its shoulders to fly through the air like a football that Jim Thorpe had just punted.

Hallam put his back against the wall of the house and reloaded the Colt yet again. Only two of the zombies were left, the ones that had been occupied with Casey and Al until now, hunched over the bodies of the hired killers, shredding and tearing with fingers and teeth. Hallam snapped the Colt's cylinder closed, took aim, and blew the head off one of them. That finally got the attention of the other. It stood up and lurched toward the house, its face smeared black with blood in the moonlight.

Hallam reached in his pocket and closed his fingers around his last four cartridges.

He felt fear rising in him as he thumbed the shells into the gun. He was operating mostly on instinct now; that was the only thing that kept him from giving in to hysteria. He closed the cylinder. If four shots weren't enough, there was still the Bowie. He told himself he would carve that damned zombie from gizzard to gullet before he'd let it chomp on him.

The Colt bucked against his palm—one, two, three, four times. Shards of bone and the slime of decayed brains flew through the air. The last zombie fell forward on the steps, twitched a few times, then lay still.

Hallam heard a faint whimpering and looked down to see Martin Larribee sitting up again, his back propped against the wall of the house.

A faint rustling sounded from the trees. Hallam's eyes jerked in that direction. If anything else came after him tonight, he'd have to rely on the Bowie to fight it off.

The rustling died away. Breathing shallowly because of the stench in the air, Hallam watched the woods, and after a few moments, his instincts told him that whatever had been out there was gone. The houngan, more than likely. But without the zombies to do his bidding, there was a limit to how much the voodoo priest could do.

Hallam blinked and rubbed the back of his left hand across his eyes. He was starting to think crazy, too.

He believed that folks could get so caught up in their religion that they'd follow somebody clear across the country for vengeance, but that didn't mean the gents he'd shot—and decapitated with his Bowie—and flat-out kicked the head off one of them—that didn't mean they were really the walking dead.

A moan of pain came from Eliza Dutton. Hallam holstered the empty Colt, slid the Bowie back into its sheath, and reached down to grab Larribee's collar. He hauled the Englishman to his feet and shook him.

"Can you drive?"

"Wh-what?"

"Can you drive the gal's car?"

Larribee shuddered. "I... I think so."

"Good. I'll put her in it, and you take her to the hospital. She's lost some blood from that arm, but she might still be all right."

"I can't do that! What will I tell them?"

"There's wolves and coyotes in these hills, even now. Tell 'em you were attacked by one or the other. Hell, you're the writer, Larribee. Make something up."

Larribee gestured shakily at the carnage around the front of the house. "But... what about all this?"

"I don't reckon I feel much like tryin' to explain it to the cops. Do you?"

A moment of silence, then, "No. No, I don't. But Eliza.... She tried to kill me."

Hallam lifted Eliza Dutton's unconscious form and started toward her car. Over his shoulder, he said, "Next time see if you can get a gal without makin' her so mad she wants to sic a zombie on you."

———

HALLAM SAW Martin Larribee only one more time. The Englishman stopped by his place to give Hallam a check and announced that he was going back to England.

"As you might expect, Hollywood holds few charms for me these days."

"What about Miss Dutton?" asked Hallam.

"I've made arrangements with a sanitarium to have her cared for. The doctors say there's a faint chance she might someday emerge from the catatonic state she's in, but they don't hold out much real hope."

Hallam shook his head. It bothered him that Eliza Dutton wouldn't face the legal consequences of what she had done. On the other hand, he didn't want to have to testify in court about the things he had seen up there off Mulholland Drive.

There was no real evidence, anyway. The cops, tipped off by the anonymous call Hallam had made to them, had found the bodies of Casey and Al, but the corpses had been so torn up their deaths had been put down to an animal attack.

There had been no sign of the zombies.

The houngan had disposed of them somehow, or maybe after a while the destroyed creatures had turned to dust or something. Hallam didn't know, didn't want to know. All that mattered was that it was over.

"Taking care of Miss Dutton in a place like that is goin' to be expensive."

"Yes, well, you see... I really do love her. I forced her to break off her engagement to Geoffrey and stay with me because I love her so much."

Hallam didn't say anything to that. Nothing he could say would mean anything to Larribee anyway.

"I'm on my way to catch a train now," Larribee went on. "When I get to New York, I'll be taking a boat for Liverpool. No offense, Mr. Hallam, but if I never see your fair country again, that will be fine with me."

Hallam grunted. "Don't reckon we'll miss you, either."

Larribee shrugged and turned to go down the walk from the foyer of Hallam's apartment building to the cab waiting at the curb. His head twitched nervously from side to side. He got into the vehicle and it drove away.

Hallam stood there long enough to see another cab go by, as if it were following the one Larribee was in. A dark face in the back seat turned toward the detective for a moment as the second cab went past. Then it was gone, too.

Martin Larribee will spend the rest of his life— however long that might be—looking over his shoulder, and probably for good cause, thought Hallam.

And for a while, Lucas Hallam might be checking his own back trail, watching the shadows, listening for the soft, shuffling tread of inhuman footsteps in the night...

It's a good thing I'm just a hard-headed old cowboy and don't believe in such nonsense, he told himself as he went inside and shut the door.

A FAST-PACED MYSTERY SET IN OLD HOLLYWOOD—WITH TWISTS AND TURNS THAT NEVER END.

It's the 1920's, and Lucas Hallam is something of a legend: a Texas Ranger turned Pinkerton agent turned Hollywood P.I. So, when the occasion arises, Hallam saddles up and rides off with Tom Mix, William S. Hart, and several other famous movie cowboys from the silent era.

Hallam doesn't think of his past often, and it's the furthest thing from his mind when he goes into Chuckwalla, California—hoping to turn the ghost town into a movie set . . . even when the two men start shooting at him.

But that's the least of Hallam's problems. His latest hired job is to protect Elton Forbes—founder of the Holiness Temple of Faith and accused of blackmail and murder.

Hallam is the only one who believes Forbes. The only question in his mind is whether he'll survive long enough to find the real killer.

Will good or evil win in the end?

AVAILABLE MARCH 2022

ABOUT THE AUTHOR

L.J. Washburn has been writing award-winning, critically acclaimed mystery, western, and historical novels for more than forty years. L.J. received the Private Eye Writers of America paperback original award and the American Mystery award for book one of the Lucas Hallam Mystery series, WILD NIGHT, and was nominated for a Spur by the Western Writers of America for a novel written with James Reasoner. Washburn also won the Western Fictioneers Peacemaker Award for the story "Charlie's Pie" and was nominated for two more stories.